Socks, Shocks and Secrets

by Leila Rasheed

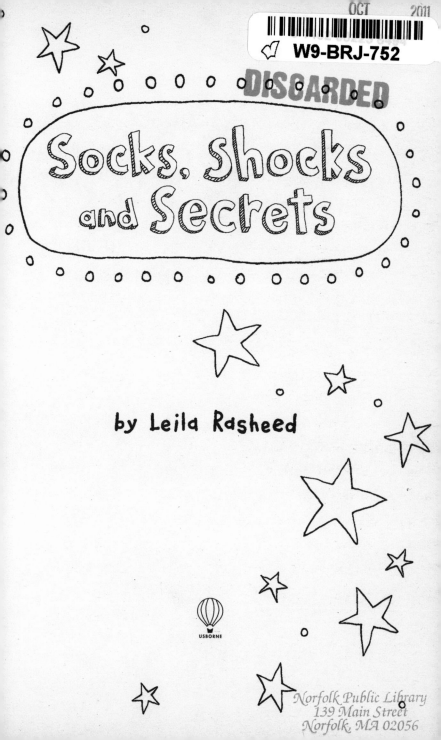

USBORNE

The
Spectacular
Second Diary
of
Bathsheba
Clarice de Trop

☆

BEING BATHSHEBA
by Bathsheba Clarice de Trop

Hello, dear readers!
This is me!!!

Bathsheba Clarice
de Trop.

Yep, that's my real name. You probably know
me from my mother's books, like *Bathsheba's
Paris Plot*, and *Bathsheba's Caribbean Crisis*.
You might think I look a little different from the
way I'm described in the books — for example,
my hair is mousy brown, not champagne blonde,
and I am not ~~pretty~~ super tall or super slim.
That is not surprising, because you see,
everything in the books is made up. I don't
have ~~many friends~~ amazingly glamorous friends
who are royalty. And I have never saved the
world or solved mysterious crimes. And I don't

go to a fancy boarding school like St. Barnaby's, because it doesn't exist. Instead, a tutor used to give me my lessons at home, which was really ~~boring~~ boring.

But all that is going to change, because — guess what — I am starting school for the very first time in just two days!! And guess which school?? Yes, that's right, on the first of September I am starting at Clotborough School in Seventh Grade. So by the time you are reading this I might be sitting at the desk next to you in math or something!!!!! Hello again!!! Take me to your leader, ha ha. (Actually, I have already met the principal, Mr. Baxter-Bix — he was nice but his face kept twitching. I think he was a little stressed by my hot-pink feather boa. If you are reading this, Mr. Baxter-Bix, I promise not to wear it to school!!!)

Well, anyway, I am not like the Bathsheba in my mother's books, and that used to make me feel sad, because I wanted to be like her.

I wanted to be super glamorous and amazing and cool. But then I got a dad and a friend and things got a lot better...except some horrible girl named Avocado stole my part in my own movie and my mother had to go to America to help make the movie ~~and I will really miss her~~ but that's okay because I don't think she'll miss me much anyway as she is always very busy. I miss Natasha, though. Natasha used to be our housekeeper but now she works for a rock star and his three children instead. She makes very good lasagna and she is the godmother of my ~~first~~ best ever friend Keisha, who edits this newspaper!!! Hello, Keisha!!!

Um, what else? Well, here are some things I am looking forward to doing at school.

☆ Joining drama club! I am so looking forward to having even a small part in a real play. And I really, really want to get into Dramarama camp next summer. I AM going to be a Movie

Star when I grow up — despite Avocado!

☆ Joining school newspaper club! My friend Keisha who edits this very newspaper is in it, and she says it's great fun.

☆ Making lots and lots of new friends!!!

☆ Midnight feasts! I know this is a day school, but they always sound so much fun in Mother's books. Maybe we could close the curtains or something? Also, I expect that something awful will happen like someone stealing the Hockey Cup because that always happens in books about school — anyway, it does in the books my mother writes. In that case, have no fear!!! I will catch the thief!!!

Spectacularly yours,
Bathsheba Clarice de Trop!!!!!!!!!

Okay, I think that is the best article I can possibly write for the Clotborough School Gazette. Now all I have to do is type it out and give it to Keisha. And hope it gets into the newspaper!

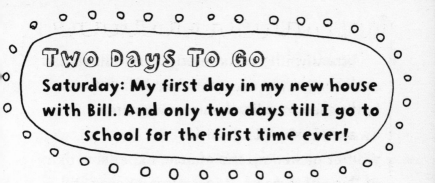

Two Days To Go

Saturday: My first day in my new house with Bill. And only two days till I go to school for the first time ever!

Dear Diary,

Here we are again! Or actually, here we are at the beginning, because of course you are not the same diary I was writing in when I was living with Mother in a Palatial Mansion in Kensington. That diary got filled up (even the cover – a lot happened over the last few months) and is under my bed in my special secrets box, waiting until I get to be a famous Movie Star, and can publish it.

You are a different diary. Quite a cheap, dull diary, because Bill – that's my dad – said we must be careful to Live Within Our Means.

Actually, if I had wanted, I could have had a nicer diary, because Mother has left me a bank account full of money for while she's away. But she didn't leave Bill one. And, well, when I picked up the mauve, expensive diary in Paperflo's today, I just remembered Bill buying a second-hand suit earlier on, and I felt awful and I put it down again...and picked up you, dear Diary! Who are gray with grayer sections, sort of like the sky at the moment. But! Not for long!! Because...I have stickers!!!

Dear Diary, welcome to your Extreme Makeover.

Sticker sticker stickery stickery stick stick stuck.

Two hours, twenty-five stickers, one tube of glitter glue and six felt tips later...

Look at you now! You are beautiful! You are Princesscular! You are shiny and glittery, with pink, blue and yellow pieces all over, and lots of gold stars, because they are the Dramarama camp logo (my best friend Keisha gave me some Dramarama stickers). And I have drawn pictures of my two ponies, Pepper and Poppy, on you!

Diary, you SHALL go to the ball.

So, what has been happening you are probably wondering? Well, a lot. Mother left to go to America this very morning and I moved into the new house with Bill. I feel a little wobbly when I think about it. I can't really imagine that Mother is really not around anymore...

But! I have to be positive, like Mother said

when she was leaving and I was nearly going to cry. And so the good thing is that I now, as from this morning, officially live with Bill, my dad!

I bet you are wondering what your new home looks like. Well, on the outside it is not very Spectacular. Our new house (Bill's house that I live in) is in a cul-de-sac, which Bill says means Bag of Bum in French. I am not sure that can be true – are governments allowed to be so rude about their streets?

From my new bedroom window I can see all the way to Taylor Tower, where Keisha lives on the twentieth floor. Our part of the neighborhood has brick houses that look all the same, sitting neatly around a grass lawn. None of it looks as scary as Mother says it is, and everyone I've met so far has been really nice.

The house where I lived with Mother was

huge; it had three living rooms, two dining rooms, eight bedrooms, four bathrooms, a swimming pool and an underground garage. This house is completely tiny – just as you are going upstairs it stops. If I stretch out my arms really far, I can touch both sides of my bedroom at once. It is actually really cool, like living in a space pod or something.

The other thing about my new house is that it has a piano stuck in the hall. This is all because the movers thought it would go in and the house was unconvinced.

Bill is very stressed about this. So I am making him a list of Good Things about having a piano stuck in the hall. Stars must always Think Positive!!!

Good things about having a piano stuck in the hall:

☆ You can hear anyone trying to break in because they play scales without meaning to.

☆ I will be able to give concerts (of *Chopsticks* and *Für Elise*) for the entire street. All I have to do is open the front door, and – ta-dah! – instant open-air festival.

☆ We will get lots of exercise climbing over and under and around it.

☆ You can jump from the middle of the stairs onto the piano, slide in your socks across the keyboard, and bounce straight through the living room door onto the sofa without hurting yourself. This makes getting downstairs faster in an emergency such as a fire.

Later: After trying and trying and trying to move the piano...

Bill has just given me a list of his own!

<u>Bad things about having a piano stuck in the hall:</u>
- We can only have very thin and active visitors, as no one else will fit around it.
- My crazy daughter keeps appearing through the living room door at jet speed because she thinks it is a great idea to use the piano keyboard as a cannonball run. I have no doubt this will soon lead to a broken leg. Or a broken sofa. Or both.
- The landlord charges for marks on the paint, and by the time we get this monster out, there will be more mark than paint. And I don't have a job yet, remember?

PS Bathsheba, you have too much stuff!

Huh. I think Bill should be less negative!

I know I have too much stuff, even though I've left loads behind (in storage, because the old house where I lived with Mother is being rented out to an American family). Mother did tell me only to choose my favorite things to take with me, but I seemed to have more favorites than non-favorites. Sigh.

These are a few of my favorite things (tra la):

☆ Seven walk-in closets' worth of clothes
☆ A piano (yes, the one stuck in the hall)
☆ A fairy castle bed (still in pieces on the lawn)
☆ A giant teddy bear of Snoopy (it used to LOOM over my crib when I was a baby. Actually I hate it, but Mother cried when I said I wanted to leave it

behind... Maybe Keisha knows
someone who would like it?)
☆ Eighty-seven other stuffed animals –
   bears, dogs, giraffes, snails, monkeys,
   pumas, etc.
☆ A bouncy castle I'd forgotten I had

And that's not counting all the books and
toys and other things that were in boxes and
boxes and boxes...

I was really astonished when I saw how
much stuff I had. Really, you don't notice it
after a while.

Actually, dear Diary, it makes me feel a
little—

Ooh, there is Keisha at the door! Got
to rollerblade, Diary – mwah, mwah, see
you later!

After being zoomy tornado-style superstar rollerbladers...

I am getting much better at rollerblading! We bladed up the path to the playground, and then we hung onto the merry-go-round and went around and around, screaming like a tornado. It was excellent fun! But very exhausting, so we had to stop after a while.

If you sit on the edge of the merry-go-round you can use one toe to sort of push yourself around, and if there are two of you, you can build up a nice rhythm and watch the sky drift in circles, and this is what we did. We talked about Dramarama summer camp. Keisha has been once already so I am sure she'll get in this year too. Oh, I hope I get in as well! I can't wait to spend a whole week in a real castle in the Wilds of Yorkshire acting and getting special training from a mystery guest star! And if you're really good – or maybe just a little crazy! – you get filmed by the camera crew and they show it on TV, on a program called *Dramarama Diaries*!

On the way back to my house, Keisha's cell buzzed to say she had a text. (I asked Bill if I could have a cell but he said NO, they give off killer rays. Keisha's phone is gorgeous – she has a pink furry cover for it with little silver charms, and her ringtone is the Dramarama theme tune.) She pulled it out and looked at it, and then she blushed, dear Diary, so pink she matched her phone!

"What is it?" I said eagerly.

"Nothing! I've got to go! Sorry! I'll see you at school, Bath." She gave me a big hug, but she didn't look me in the eyes as she said goodbye. And then she went zooming up the hill on her rollerblades!

Very WEIRD, dear Diary.

I wonder who on earth could have texted her?

My first ever bedtime in my new house!

Well, this is my first night in my new house. It's a weird feeling, dear Diary. It feels as if I'm camping out, only it's not, it's real.

After dinner (chicken stir-fry, yum) Bill and me watched television for a while. I never do that with Mother, because she is always too stressed to relax. I didn't think about anything else while *Dramarama Diaries* was on, because I was too busy hoping that the one with blue hair would get to act Romeo, but as soon as it finished, I sort of woke up and looked around and thought, *Hmm, it is probably bedtime.*

Usually I am not exactly eager to go to bed, but tonight was different. I wanted to get it over with as quickly as possible so it wouldn't be the first time any longer. And I wanted time to settle into my new room and make sure I could get from the light switch to the covers quickly in case it turned out to be the sort of bedroom that was scary in the dark. Besides, Bill was already yawning.

"Well," I said, "goodnight!"

"Do you, uh, want a bedtime story or something?" Bill said nervously.

"I'm not a baby!"

"Yeah, sorry, sorry. Just…you know. I wouldn't want you to feel like I wasn't being a real dad or something…"

"It's okay, Bill," I said kindly, "I've got a book."

"Oh good," he said, sounding very relieved. "Well, goodnight then."

"Night."

"Goodnight."

We sort of bobbed at each other like polite Japanese gentlemen, and then I scurried off upstairs to bed.

I am lying here feeling low and miserable, dear Diary. (But glad I have a flashlight so I can write in you!)

I miss Mother. And I miss Natasha too, because actually it was Natasha who used to do my bedtime story and tuck me in for ages (until I got too old, of course) because Mother was hardly ever there at bedtime. Oh, I hope Mother is okay, flying over the Atlantic. Or is it the Pacific? I can never remember.

In the middle of the day there are never so many things to worry about as there are at night. I think they creep out of the shadows or something. Maybe the shadows are a Dark Portal to a Land of Demons... Ooh, I had better stop thinking scary stuff right now. Stop. Stop. Stop.

The thing is, everything is so new. Even the shadows are new, differently-scary shadows than in my old bedroom. And Mother is not here, and neither is Natasha, only Bill is here.

I keep thinking how I hardly know Bill really, because of him not being around for years. What if we find out we don't like each other?

What happens if Bill decides he doesn't want a daughter after all?

I sort of feel, right now, as if I would like to just run away and go back in time to when I lived with Mother and didn't have to go to school, and everything felt safe and normal. Only I can't. And I don't *really* want to. I know it is just the new shadows doing my thinking for me.

But what if Bill feels like running away from having a daughter? He could. He's a grown-up. Grown-ups can do whatever they want.

What if he abandons me? And Mother is in America so she can't come and get me?

Oh dear, oh dear. Must Think Positive!

Must think about nice things! Like...school.

I am SO looking forward to school. All the exciting things seem to happen to Bathsheba in the books when she's at school. Like rescuing her best friend from certain death! Or finding out there's a princess in disguise hiding in the gym. Or the sanatorium burning down and having to escape on knotted sheets made into a rope!

And of course, when she's at school, Bathsheba in the books has all her millions of friends to help in her exciting adventures.

Ooh, I can't wait to get to school and start making friends! I want enough friends so that I can have an entourage, which is basically all the friends you can fit into a limousine.

...I know that shadow over there looks particularly dark and loomy, but actually it is the closet, and inside the closet is my new school uniform. It looks so cool! It's green, with yellow and black stripes on the tie. Yes! I even have a tie! I can't do it up, though. Bill has been trying to show me, but I just keep getting my fingers in a knot.

So there, dear Diary. Shadows may look unpleasant, but usually there's something nice inside them. Now I can get some sleep. Only one more bedtime until school starts!

o   o   o   o   o   o   o   o   o

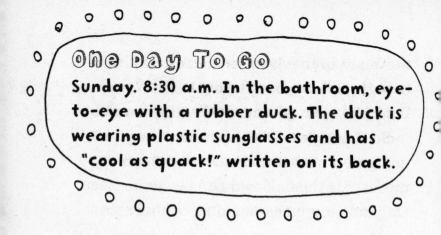

One Day To Go

Sunday. 8:30 a.m. In the bathroom, eye-to-eye with a rubber duck. The duck is wearing plastic sunglasses and has "cool as quack!" written on its back.

Well, this morning I got up at the usual time, did my Movie Star exercises (three different kinds of pose and two smirks) and then went off to the bathroom. Only to find it locked. And male singing and shower noises coming from inside!

This would NEVER happen in Mother's house. I have my own bathroom there. I stood outside holding my ecru towel and my hot-pink toothbrush, not knowing what to do, and feeling as if I was going to cry.

It was just one more new thing after another.

And then the door opened, and Bill sort of surged out on a wave of shaving cream.

"Waiting for the bath, Bath? Ha ha." He looked at my face. "Okay, sorry, not very funny I know, but that's the best I can do this early in the morning..."

"I wish to wash," I said mournfully.

He looked worriedly at me, and then seemed to decide I was better off left alone.

"Good idea. Into the shower with you, spit-spot, clean machine!"

???

Honestly, being a dad seems to make people talk utter nonsense.

It did make me smile, though. I think it *will* be good, living with Bill.

I don't know where the duck came from. It wasn't there before.

Life is full of such little mysteries.

After breakfast, feeling much much better!!! (Only one more breakfast before school!)

Okay, today I am going to explore our Baggy Bum street. On my rollerblades. Dressed in a tutu.

I told Bill this and he said, "Why a tutu?"

Why not???

Tutus are charming!

He said, "I don't think Stanley and Livingstone or Captain Scott wore tutus on their explorations."

"Well," I said, "in that case, those people, whoever they were, had no dress sense!"

So there!

First break from exploration: eating a banana to keep up my strength. ✳ ⑥

So, dear Diary:

On our street there are ten houses. Some of them have flowers in their front yards and one of them has an ice-cream truck! There is a white dumpster in the road that is full of broken stuff. I think the people in that house have just moved in and are fixing it up. I rollerbladed around outside for a while, but they don't seem to have any children my age, just teenagers.

The lady next door wears a sari. She has a little boy who pedals around on a tricycle, looking stunned. Their house smells gorgeously of cooking. I DEFINITELY want to make friends with them. I have put it on my TO DO list.

Almost opposite us is a scary house. I have

already heard people shouting in there and it is not even lunchtime yet. They have heaps of dog poop in their yard. I can hear dogs barking right now.

They do not sound like the kind of dogs that would fit in a handbag.

I don't think even their bark would fit in a handbag – it would have to be a really big handbag. Maybe with bars and chains on it to stop the bark from getting out and savaging people.

Back on the baggy bum exploration trail...

Ooh, dear Diary, I met a native! I mean, a neighbor.

I was just rollerblading along singing, tra la, and enjoying wearing my ecru tutu and my stripey mauve and vermilion leggings,

and my new bright blue jacket that Mother
bought me as a going-away present. I do
think I was looking fairly Spectacular.

Anyway, this ghost rose up from the
dumpster, and I screamed and lost control of
the rollerblades, and sort of drifted horribly
right – crash! – into him. You know when
rabbits are caught in the headlights of a car
and they WANT to run away but they just
can't make their legs work right in time and
squash? Well, it was like that.

Clang I went, into the dumpster and into
the ghost, who was not actually a ghost but
a boy, but he looked like a ghost. The ghost
confusion happened because he was wearing
big black sunglasses (not in a Movie Star sort
of way, just in a Big Black Sunglasses sort of
way), and he had pale red hair, a pale shiny
face, big white ears with black earphones
plugged into them, a white tracksuit that
made him look even more pale and skinny,

white sneakers and his tracksuit bottoms were tucked into his socks, which were black. So it was kind of like these big black sunglasses and earphones and skinny black ankles were floating in front of me, as the rest of him kind of faded out against the white dumpster. I blinked. He faded back in again.

"Hello," I said. Then I realized he couldn't hear me because he was plugged into his earphones, so I waved. Then I realized he was wearing sunglasses and probably couldn't see me either.

Dear Diary, I had no idea how to communicate with him. I considered sort of elegantly tripping and falling onto the wire coming from his earphones so they pulled out, but then I thought what if he is a Criminal Element like Mother keeps going on about (he did look really weird) and attacks me?

So I did a little dance instead, to fill the awkward silence.

"Um, er, are you, er—" he said, or rather, stuttered. The way fans do with celebrities. His knees were knocking. I sighed. It is so difficult being recognized all the time. I mean, it probably is. I have been told that it is.

"Yes," I said, "I am Bathsheba Clarice de Trop. THE Bathsheba Clarice de Trop." I did another little dance, because I was rather proud of managing to do the first one without falling off my rollerblades.

He made a gurgling noise. "Are you wonderful?" he said. "I'm Hunderchunk. I mean – me Hunderchunk. You Wonderchunk." Then he covered his face with his hands and moaned, "Sorry! I mean, I'm Nathan!"

I stared at him suspiciously, wondering if this was his normal behavior.

Then he started talking again, which I thought was hardly fair because it was my turn, so I started talking over him. And then there was an indistinct roar from inside the scary house, and Nathan sort of flattened his ears like ponies do in a crisis and disappeared back inside the dumpster.

I banged on the side a couple of times, but there was no answer, so I rollerbladed off home. Which is where I am now, dear Diary, and it is almost lunchtime.

Keisha and Bev, her mother, are coming over for lunch.

Mother *never* makes lunch. She used to just ask Natasha to Whip Up a Little Something, which usually meant macrobiotic, or quail's eggs, depending on her diet.

Bill has made cheese and tomato sandwiches. Yum yum yum! And he has borrowed a lot of cookbooks from Bev. Bev is really nice. She helped Bill find this house. She is round and smiley, and a nurse, which is a useful thing to be.

Keisha's dad is dead. But when I look at Keisha's photo of him, I can tell he was really nice too. Poor Keisha. I am so lucky to still have a dad. I hope Bill thinks he is lucky to have a daughter, too!

Lunchtime! Last lunch before school — my next lunch will be at school!!

We had a nice lunch with Keisha and Bev. We all leaned on the piano as if it was a cocktail bar, and had sandwiches and orange juice.

Bev said, "That playground is an eyesore. We can't get the council to do anything." She waved behind us to the playground where me and Keisha had been tornado-ing yesterday. It's true, it is really rusty and broken in places.

"Maybe try again?" said Bill. "We could get together and write them a letter."

"I could write it!" said Keisha. "I learned all about protests in school newspaper club last year."

"You'll have enough to do with your schoolwork and all your after-school clubs this year, young lady," said Bev. Although Bev is really round and smiley, she can also be very stern, in a Mother of Steel kind of way. She had a stern look right then. "You don't need any more things distracting you from your school lessons. You're not thinking of applying to Dramarama camp again this year, are you?"

Keisha sort of shrieked, and I went, "Oh please, Bev, please, you can't stop her from going to Dramarama camp!"

"Okay, calm down! I didn't say you *couldn't* apply!" Bev gave Keisha a hug. "Just so long as you're not distracted from schoolwork, that's all."

"I won't be," promised Keisha, and I said, "She won't be!" Me and Keisha made relieved faces at each other over the piano.

Eek, dear Diary! I hate it when you suddenly get reminded of the total power parents have to ruin everything for you. (Not that Bev would do that on purpose! She's super nice.)

After Bev and Keisha have gone...

I am looking out of the window now and thinking about how much stuff I have.

It does feel a little funny that in my house there are six games consoles and three TVs and eighty-seven stuffed animals and an enormous dollhouse and everything else, whereas outside there is a broken playground. It makes things feel a little...out of balance. Like my house is greedier than all the other houses. You know, it tried to swallow a piano and couldn't manage it.

A fairy castle bed is a little babyish for a twelve year old.

Ooh, someone at the door!!

Wow, well that was weird – it was the ghost boy again. I opened the door and he said nervously, "Hello, I'm Nathan."

I said, "So what? I mean, I know."

What is it with this boy? It seems as if I can't make sense when I talk to him! And he doesn't seem able to make sense at all period.

He said, "Oh," and looked very disappointed, and turned to leave. And then he turned back again (nearly tripping over his shoelaces) and muttered, "Here," and shoved something at me. I took it sort of automatically, and I was still staring at him thinking how strange he was and also feeling bad in case I'd sounded rude, so it wasn't until

a couple of moments later that I looked
at it and went, "Eeeek!!!!!" Because, dear
Diary, it was a bomb!!!

I rushed into the house to show Bill, but
then I rushed out again because I thought,
*What if it goes off and blows up the house
which isn't ours but the landlord's?* Bill came
rushing out after me.

"Bath, what are you screaming about?"

"A bomb, a bomb!" I shrieked, waving it
at him.

"Nonsense, Bathsheba," he said, very calmly
taking it off me, "it's just a circuit board.
Something that makes electrical
things work – looks like one
from an old computer."

"Oh!" I looked at it more
carefully. It did look like a
bomb ought to: there were all
wires sticking out of it, and it
looked menacing.

We went back into the house. Bill peered at the circuit board in a manly sort of way, as if he knew what it did. "Where did you get it?" he asked.

"Some weird boy named Nathan gave it to me," I said. I looked up and there he was at the window, with his face pressed to the glass and his sunglasses still on.

"There he is!" I shrieked, grabbing Bill's arm. By the time he had turned around, of course, Nathan had run off.

Dear Diary, I can't get the image of his looming dark glasses and floating skinny ankles out of my mind. Looming and floating. Floating and looming. Looming and floating and floaming and looting.

It is probably an Omen.

I hope it is not a bad one for my first day at school tomorrow…

I have put the circuit board under my bed.

9 p.m. at night, after Dramarama Diaries has finished. And my book has finished. And there is nothing to do but think. ☆

6

I really miss Mother right now. She cried before she went. I've never seen her cry before, or hardly ever.

She gave me lots of good advice about being Positive and Sociable and Networking so as to Build my Profile (or something, dear Diary, I stopped understanding after a while), and she made Bill promise to e-mail every single evening, and me to e-mail as much as possible, and then she sniffed and wiped her eyes and said, "Good heavens, is that the time? I'll miss my plane." And then she hugged me, and got into her limo and went. And I was just going to cry myself when the movers came up and said, "Um, we've got a little problem," and it turned out the piano was stuck in the hall, so there was no time for it.

Sigh. I miss Natasha, too.

On her last day, I gave her a Death by Chocolate cake with six candles, one for every year she worked for us. We had a little party in the kitchen while Mother was out. I wanted to have silly string, but Natasha said not while she was still responsible for cleaning it up.

I said, "Natasha, you will miss me, won't you?"

She gave me a big hug and said, "Of course I will, Butterball. I'll come and see you as often as possible."

I hope the rock star's children are horrible. I mean not so horrible that Natasha gets upset. Just horrible enough so she doesn't start liking them more than me!

10 p.m. Bedtime.

Bill put his head around the door after I'd gone to bed. I hid you very quickly, Diary! I am not supposed to be writing but getting a Good Night's Rest instead, because of school (SCHOOL!!!) tomorrow.

"Sleep well, Bath," he said. "It's a new start tomorrow for both of us! There's a job center next to the school, so I can go there right after dropping you off. Good, huh? I'm going to get a job, and this time I won't mess up. I promise!"

"I won't mess up either," I said. "I'm going to be the best at school, and the best at drama club so I get into Dramarama camp, and have millions of friends, and, and, and—"

"Make sure you remember to have fun too," he said, laughing.

But all that stuff WILL be fun, dear Diary!!! Obviously.

o   o   o   o   o   o   o   o   o

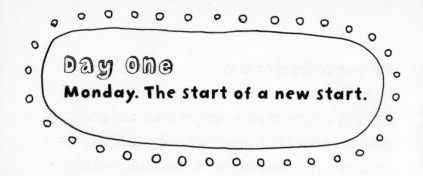

Day One
Monday. The start of a new start.

Dear Diary,

I am about to go to school!!!!

Oops, sorry, I didn't mean to get milk on you. I'm just having my breakfast and writing in you at the same time, and sometimes the spoon gets mixed up with the pen.

I have been awake for AGES.

I got up really early and opened my new curtains in my new bedroom and looked out of my new window at my new world and thought about going to my new school and felt SO excited I could hardly stop myself from bouncing on the bed. I got out the map of the school that Keisha made for me the other week (with stickers to show where the different classrooms are), and found the locker room and the science lab and the cafeteria. I put on my school uniform and took it off and put it on again with the buttons done up differently and other tights, and packed my school bag (ecru with hot pink stars) and unpacked it, and stuck Dramarama stickers on my school shoes, and then I heard Bill groaning from the other bedroom and going, "Bathsheba, for heaven's sake go back to sleep, it's four a.m." So I did. But now I am awake again and full of cornflakes and I'm off, dear Diary, I am really going to SCHOOL!!!!

Oh WOW.

I feel as if I have a happy balloon inside me and it is yearning to get out.

School is going to be amazing.

I am going to love every single moment of it.

Bill is in a really good mood too, now he is actually awake. He is all enthusiastic and bright-eyed – he reminds me of one of those squirrels in the park near where I used to live. He has been dancing around the kitchen singing along to the Golden Oldies radio station. (Not that squirrels do that. Unless you feed them too many Tic Tacs.) He also did my tie for me – hooray! I don't think I will ever be able to do it right, it keeps coming out lop-eared.

Oh, and guess what else: this morning in the shower, I turned the rubber duck over, and on the bottom it says MADE BY QUACKO PRODUCTIONS.

From now on, my new word for weird is going to be QUACKO.

Monday evening. My first evening as a Seventh Grader! Wow, I feel So grown-up!

Dear Diary,

I have just had my first ever day at school!!!

I bet you are dying to know what it was like. After all, diaries don't go to school. (Although maybe they should. They could learn the best ways to keep secrets. Or how to decipher messy handwriting.)

Bill and me walked up through the neighborhood. Everyone always says first impressions count, and I REALLY wanted to get it right, so I practiced doing Movie Star greetings. You know, where you introduce yourself and your teeth twinkle.

"Hi," I was muttering to myself as I walked along, "I'm Bathsheba!!!" and, "Hi!!! I'm Bath!!!" and even, "The name's de Trop. Bathsheba Clarice de Trop," when suddenly

I realized I was completely surrounded by children who were all around my age or older, and who were all wearing the same uniform as me. I don't know where they came from, they just seemed to explode out of nowhere; busloads of them appearing and bounding around, and they were mostly shouting and laughing and seemed to all know each other and be totally okay with throwing each other's school bags around and shouting at each other and pushing their phones in each other's faces and stuff. And then there was the school at the end of the road. And it was FULL of people.

I suddenly wished I had gone to America instead, after all. I got this awful down-down-down feeling inside me, as if the happy balloon had started sinking the other way. I think I must have stopped walking so fast, because Bill turned to me and said, "What's the matter, Bath? Aren't you feeling well?"

Dear Diary, I so wanted to say, "No, I am Gravely Sick, take me to a doctor instead of to school," but I knew Keisha was waiting for me in front of the school gates, because she promised she would, and I couldn't let her down, so I said, "I'm fine!!!" but it came out a little like a mouse shrieking. We were almost at the gates by then, and I couldn't see Keisha anywhere. I kept thinking, *Will I have to go in all alone?* and, *What happens if I get lost and they never find me again?* and, *What if I get trampled flat and they have to send me home in an envelope?* which seemed more and more likely as some big boys jumped off the bus and shoved past us.

Bill looked at me very worriedly. "Do you want me to come in with you?" he asked.

I didn't know what to say. Of course I didn't want to go in with my dad and look like a baby, but I didn't think I could manage to walk in there alone, even if I tried. No one told me school was so BIG. (I mean, they did, but not really. Keisha's map is not to scale.)

Thank heavens for Keisha!!!

"Hi, Bath," she said, popping up behind me out of nowhere. "This is so cool! I can't believe you're finally here! Come with me, I'll show you everything."

"Bye, Dad," I squeaked, and suddenly it was my first day at school and I couldn't wait!! Keisha grabbed my arm, and rushed off through the gates with me following, and it wasn't until much later that I realized I'd called Bill "Dad" to his face for the very first time.

Inside, it was also complete chaos, with boys bouncing off the walls and girls braiding each other's hair and shrieking at each other, and a few teachers sort of surfing along on the top of the crowd as if they didn't really know how they'd gotten there. One of the teachers had a blue Mohawk, which I was not expecting!

Keisha showed me the lockers, and put her things away. "You look really nervous," she said. "Don't worry, you'll be fine! Everything's a little crazy at the start of a new school year. Hi, Alicia." She nodded, not very enthusiastically, to a girl with neat cornrows, who was putting her things away too. There was a rolled-up copy of YAY! magazine sticking out of her bag.

"Hi, Keisha," said Alicia, with a really big, sharp smile. I looked at her curiously and she stared back at me. But the next thing I knew, we were being whirled up the corridor like leaves in a stream of green uniforms. I couldn't help feeling panicky.

"What if people don't like me?" I asked Keisha. "What if they ignore me or bully me or—"

"Of course they won't! Why should they? Anyway, they all know your mother's books –

so they'll be interested in you. You'll have more friends than me soon."

I could not believe *that*, because she seemed to know every other girl we passed as we went along the corridor, and they all seemed to know her back, and it was just "Hi, Keisha!", "Hey, Keisha, how was your summer? I love your new bag!", "Keish! How's it going, girl?" and so on, as we went deeper and deeper and DEEPER into this complete maze of a building which kept on sprouting new corridors everywhere (and all painted a rather horrible shade of green). I just kept my arm hooked into Keisha's as tightly as possible. I wondered what would happen if I got lost and whether anyone would ever be able to find me again or whether I would just wander the yucky green corridors going *help, help* until I was too old for school and they rounded me up and pushed me out of the door with all the other new grown-ups.

And just as I was thinking that, Keisha opened the door of a classroom that looked exactly like all the others, and cried, "Here we are!"

"Keisha!!" chorused just about every girl in there. I had a sort of wild impression of uniforms and nail polish and shampoo smell, and then they stampeded at us like dogs do sometimes when they haven't seen you for just long enough to remember how much they like you. Everyone hugged Keisha, and I got hugged too, in the confusion. All the boys were sort of hanging out looking tough and bored by the windows, but I could see they were all peeking over at us.

Oh yes, dear Diary, there are BOYS in my class!!! Obviously, I knew there would be. But I'd sort of forgotten. I remembered then that I didn't know any boys at all. What on earth are you supposed to say to them? I don't know anything about football!

"Hi, everyone," said Keisha, "Hilucyhianna hihannahhipreetahijulie-louisehichanelle hivictoria!" Or at least that's what it sounded like. "This is Bathsheba!" She pushed me forward. "She's new, and she's in our class!"

Some of the boys said hello, but most of them ignored me, and the girls sort of backed off and looked me up and down. "Hello," they said politely.

I sort of burbled something and Keisha said, "Ow, Bath, let go of my arm, you're really squeezing!" Everyone laughed, but in a nice way, and I laughed too and let go. And then the girl named Alicia was pushing through the group and STARING at me.

"You're Bathsheba Clarice de Trop? THE Bathsheba Clarice de Trop? From the books? I mean, I heard the rumor you were coming here but I totally didn't believe it was true..." She looked me up and down, and I had a horrible worried feeling as she said,

"You're not exactly like in the books."

I opened my mouth to explain, but just at that moment the most awful noise, sort of halfway between a fire alarm and a screaming zombie alien warrior, went off right in my ear. Everyone started shouting and running around, and Alicia clapped her hands over her ears, and I stood there wondering if I was going bonkers. The noise went on and on and ON and then stopped, and I took a big gulp because it had sort of made me forget how to breathe, and I said to Keisha, "What was THAT?"

She grinned. "Oh, just the bell. You'll get used to it."

Dear Diary, that bell just kept going off. And on. And on and on and off and on. Until I felt like my head was in a food processor. Basically school is like a game show – as soon as the bell goes off (or on) you have to STOP

WHAT YOU ARE DOING AND RUN AROUND SHRIEKING. I think the idea is to get into the right classroom for the next lesson before the bell stops ringing, but no one ever manages it and I am not sure what you win if you do manage it – maybe homework, which does not sound worth it.

I met some of the teachers, and they are all a little quacko like Mr. Baxter-Bix, but Keisha says that is normal, and that is how you know they are teachers. Miss Kinsey, the English teacher, is very quacko! I have only had her for one class but I can already tell that she could be really strict if she wanted to be. She has neat gray hair and neat gray glasses, and she is the only teacher in the whole school who wears a suit. It is sort of thick wool full of lots of colors that all add up to gray.

Miss Kinsey is also in charge of school newspaper club. If she doesn't like my "Being

Bathsheba" article, it won't go in the paper!

Oh, I hope she likes it! I worked really, really hard on it!

The other classes we had today were French, science and math. It was really weird being in a class full of people, because I've only ever had lessons at home with just me and a tutor. Before, I could ask questions whenever I didn't understand something, but here there's so much else going on that the teacher doesn't always notice me not understanding. I felt a little drowned! Thank heavens Keisha was there to whisper explanations to me.

Science was SO cool, because it was just like science lessons in Mother's books. With Miss Kipper, my tutor, we sometimes did experiments in the kitchen, but here they have a special science room with special science chairs and a special science smell! You even get to wear white coats like a mad professor!

Math was so NOT cool. I have never been good at math, and sadly I don't think I am going to start being good at it just because I am now at a real school and am in Seventh Grade with a best friend and everything. The math teacher is Miss Notman. It isn't that she is horrible – no, she seems nice – but she says things like, "If a = b, then y?" And what is one supposed to answer to that, dear Diary?

When I came out of school, Bill was waiting for me, and he said, "Well? How was it??"

I played it cool and said, "How was what?"

He laughed. "How was school, of course!"

So I gave him a HUGE grin, and jumped up and down, and shouted, "It was totally SPECTACULAR, Dad!!!"

But...

Ooh, Bill has just yelled upstairs that Mother

is on the phone! Dear Diary, I will explain
BUT later.

Half an hour later.

Oh dear, Mother was really irritated when she
heard about the piano. She kept going, "It's a
Bechstein!" I said, "*Quoi*, Mother? *Quoi*?"
(*Quoi* is my first French word – I learned it at
school today. It means, "What?" and sounds a
little ducky, which is why I remembered it.)

"It's very expensive! It's a Bechstein!"

"A *quoi*, Mother?"

"A Bechstein!"

"*Quoi? Quoi?* Quack?"

"Bathsheba, stop being ridiculous and put
Bill on the phone immediately."

And then I could just hear her jabbering
away on the other end of the line and Bill
going, "No... No... Yes... No, but... Yes," and

I thought, probably this is what it was like
when they were living together and no
wonder they split up. And then I started
feeling wobbly, thinking of how far away
Mother was, on the other end of that long,
long, long phone line, and I wanted to run
and grab the phone off Bill and shout,
"Mother, I love you!" down the phone, but it
was too late, because he had hung up.

I hardly told her anything about school.

She told me a lot about Hollywood, though.
It does sound amazing! But I'm glad I'm here
– with my best friend, and my new school,
and my dad.

Later.   ✳ ⑥

Anyway, dear Diary. I was going to tell you
about the BUT.

School was SPECTACULAR.

That is what I told Bill. And it is true. But there is another truth. Not such a good one.

School is SCARY.

I don't want to tell Bill, because he will worry. And if I tell Keisha it will sound as if I am not grateful to her for being such a wonderful friend and looking after me all day. Which she did fabulously!

But, Diary, despite Keisha, all day I felt totally terrified and lost. I just didn't know anything, or anyone, and it was all completely, totally new. NOTHING made sense.

Why aren't we allowed to run in the corridors?

Why do we have to only wear one kind of shoes?

Why do the bigger kids just think they can push you over?

Why do we have to have our shirts tucked in?

And there were so many people!!! I have never seen so many people all in the same place before. I mean I have, like at one of Mother's book signings or something, but not when I am supposed to be MAKING FRIENDS with all of them and totally failing. And when they have all known each other since they were about three. And I haven't.

Then there are the boys. This is the first time I have really met any boys and I think they are quacko. They run around zooming. What do you do with them? What are they for??? Okay, there is one nice looking one; his name is Rafiq. He is tall and plays basketball, and all the girls drool over him when he goes bounding up the basketball court like a pony with his floppy chocolate brown mane – I mean, hair – bouncing.

...Bill is a boy too, I suppose. He isn't as quacko as the boys at school, but he still does things like leave his socks on the fridge. And he yells at the TV when football is on, even though I can't see anything to yell about, just a lot of little people in colored jerseys running around on the field as usual. He is so not like Mother! She never yells at the TV, in fact she doesn't watch TV at all because she never has time.

Oh, I will probably get around to understanding boys one day, but right now I have enough to do keeping on top of school. It is like trying to ride a bucking bronco or something! I keep thinking I know what is going on and then everything flips around and it seems you have to be in three places at once to stay on top of things! I hardly bounced at all, all day, and that is not like me. I got bounced ON instead. Huh! School is certainly Spectacular. The trouble is, it is more Spectacular than I am!!! Tomorrow I am definitely going to try being more bouncy.

o   o   o   o   o   o   o   o   o

Today I found out more about the people in my class. Most of them seem really nice and friendly. But, there's only one really REALLY popular girl. Guess who? No – not Keisha, though of course everyone likes her too! It's Alicia, the girl with the YAY! magazine who I saw yesterday.

I am a little shy with Alicia, dear Diary, because she is like a real-life Bathsheba from the books. She is so clever and can do everything well (even math!). She makes her school uniform look cool and special by customizing it with markers (on the white parts of the cuff) and nail polish (on the buttons). I think I will have to do that too!

She is a little stand-offish and isn't friends with just anyone. Her two special friends are Chanelle and Davina. Chanelle and Davina are the two prettiest girls in the class, dear Diary. They have matching hair and nail polish. Alicia isn't so pretty, but she has very sharp eyes. They are like tweezers. They pick up on everything.

Chanelle said, "Everyone calls us Alicia's Angels!" And Davina explained how their special symbol is an angel, because Alicia's middle name is Angelica. They have this thing of drawing angels on their hands and notebooks and stuff. No one else in our grade is allowed to wear anything with an angel on it, or draw angels on their notebooks, even. Fairies are okay, or People with Wings, but not angels. Angels are just for Alicia and Chanelle and Davina.

Oh, and the people in my class found out more about *me* this afternoon too! Everyone wanted to know why I'd left St. Barnaby's. Alicia looked at me really funnily when I explained St. Barnaby's wasn't real.

"You *are* famous, right?" she said.

"Well, yes. I mean no. I mean, Mother is."

"You really do have a huge house somewhere though, right?" said Davina. "It's not just a lie like St. Barnaby's?"

"It's not a *lie*," I said a little irritably, because Mother doesn't lie. "It's a story – that's different. Fifi and Aurelia and Brad are made-up. And I've never really had adventures like Mother writes about."

"So what is real?" asked Alicia.

"Well, I am!"

"Yeah, yeah. But what else? Do you really have a swimming pool with your logo on the bottom? And seven walk-in closets? Or is that all lies too?"

"No! I do have a huge house. With a swimming pool, and everything else. You can see it," I added, feeling as if I had to stick up for my life a little, "when Mother comes back from America."

"Oh, I believe you!" she said, which was funny because she hadn't sounded as if she did at all. "Well, Bathsheba, I have always wanted to be friends with a real celebrity! I am so glad you've come to Clotborough!"

Everyone was staring at us!! I am *soooo* excited, dear Diary. Only two days at school and I am already mixing with the Glamorous Set!

Only Keisha didn't look very pleased.

"We're going to be late for school newspaper club," she said, and pulled me after her. Alicia followed.

School newspaper club happens in the computer room. This is full of...yep, computers. In fact, everyone went "OOOHHH" when we went in and saw them, because they are brand new and super sleek – it is a little like walking into Space Command Central or something. They sort of glint and murmur, as if they are talking about you in numbers behind your back, and then they all whirr together unexpectedly as if they are laughing at you for not being a computer like them.

But before we even got into the computer room, I also met the scariest girl in the school! We had just gotten to the door when we heard shouting from inside.

"Wow!" I said to Keisha. "Who's that?"

"Oh, Hannah Lumb from the Ninth Grade. She's always shouting. Watch out—!"

A good thing she pulled me out of the way, dear Diary, because out of the room charged a big girl who looked like an angry rhinoceros, and she almost trampled me underfoot!

Miss Kinsey came out after her, saying,

"Really, Hannah! This belligerence is totally inappropriate!" (Which I think means "Calm down!") It didn't work. Hannah made a howling noise and punched the wall so hard that she made a hole in it. And then she stormed off.

"That wall could have been someone's head!" said Alicia. "She is *soooo* violent. Of course, they say that her family—"

"Come in, girls," interrupted Miss Kinsey, "and, Alicia, that's enough gossip, thank you!"

And then we didn't have time to talk anymore, because it was time for school newspaper club!

Miss Kinsey is not too happy about the new computers. She jumps whenever they whirr. Keisha had to show her how to use some of the programs.

"So," Miss Kinsey said, when we were finally all settled down (there are only ten of us, but that makes it even harder to decide where to sit because there's more choice!), "this year, we have these new and highly expensive computers with which we are expected to take the *Clotborough School Gazette* online, forging boldly down the information superhighway into a bright new future. However, I rejoice to tell you that we have a stay of execution. The next issue will be printed on paper, as usual."

"But we *can* use the new computers?" said a boy eagerly.

"Oh, I suppose so. If you must."

"Cool!" said everyone.

(It IS cool, dear Diary. The computers make it really easy to make the newspaper look good and professional. You can add in photos and pictures and graphs and things, and make all the headings different colors. Like mauve, and gamboge, and bright blue.)

"I want to be editor!" said Alicia. "I've got loads of good ideas!"

"You know we already decided that Keisha should stay on as editor. You can vote again in the spring."

"But I want to vote now," said Alicia, making a face.

"Democracy does not work that way," said Miss Kinsey sternly.

So Keisha is still editor, hooray! And, even more hooray – my "Being Bathsheba" article is going in! Although I'm not sure Miss Kinsey really liked it. She said "Your style has energy, Bathsheba, but your article is a little...tabloid-friendly, don't you think?"

I was just going to feel upset and disappointed when Keisha saved the day. She said, "But, Miss Kinsey, Bath being at our school really is NEWS! Just think how many new people will read the *Gazette* when they see Bathsheba Clarice de Trop on the front page."

The front page! I hadn't even imagined that. Keisha is amazing.

Miss Kinsey shook her head, but she said, "It's true that the circulation is in decline. And I admit Bathsheba's article is more interesting than the cafeteria renovations, which is the other option..."

So thanks to Keisha, "Being Bathsheba" is not just going in, it's going to be on the front page of the *Clotborough School Gazette*'s next issue!

o   o   o   o   o   o   o   o   o

So, dear Diary,

How do you like my new, customized school uniform?

I have colored over the yellow parts of my tie with gold marker pen. And it seems you are allowed to wear one simple necklace, so I am wearing my red coral chain that Mother got me when we went to Bermuda. She does not often buy me presents herself – not because she is mean, but I don't think she ever has the time. Natasha always used to buy my clothes and games and things, and she always has to remind Mother when it is my birthday. I don't feel upset by that, though, because to be honest Mother forgets

Christmas unless she puts it in her Blackberry.

I haven't forgotten you either, dear Diary!

I have made you a bookmark out of paper, shaped like a school tie (it also has gold marker detail). So no one will be able to throw you out for not being in uniform!

After school, but before dinner.

The boy with the floating socks is in my class!!! He just turned up today. Alicia says his name is Nathan Hunderchunk and he is quacko!!!!

"All the Hunderchunks are crazy," she told me at break. "It runs in the family. His big brother, Jason, actually got expelled a few years ago!"

"No!" I was really shocked.

"Yeah! Jason was even worse than Hannah Lumb. My cousin – she's at college now – was in his grade and she says he actually tried to burn down the gym!"

I felt my mouth make a big O. I hope
I never meet Jason Hunderchunk!

I don't know why Nathan wasn't at school
before. Alicia says he sometimes misses school
but he always turns up eventually. He doesn't
answer any questions except in IT when he
goes crazy typing all kinds of things and by
the end of the class he has invented a new
computer game or something. He looks even
stranger in a school uniform; he has had a very
short haircut since I saw him last and now his
head floats on top of his school uniform like
the ghost of a pickled onion.

And guess what else???

When I opened my desk at the end of math...
THERE WAS ANOTHER CIRCUIT BOARD
IN THERE!!!!!

I handed it in to Lost and Found. The
teacher on duty looked at me strangely, but
she took it without protesting.

After having beaten Bill twice at Pictionary (I don't think he is really trying). ✱ ☆

I don't know what to think about Nathan Hunderchunk.

He doesn't seem to have any friends. Which is sad, and I feel sorry for him. But at the same time, if his brother is that crazy, what must he be like? I am also a little scared of him as he is clearly quacko, what with all the circuit board stuff.

And there is something else, which might make me sound a little selfish – but I can tell you, dear Diary, because you are my friend and will not judge me. (Also, you are only a book.)

I sort of feel that, if I were to be friendly to Nathan Hunderchunk, then everyone at school could start thinking I was really quacko too. Not Keisha! But other people. Who don't know me so well.

I'm really scared that people in this school might not like me. After all, they have all had a year to get used to each other and make friends, before I ever arrived.

I don't want to go all the way through to the end of school with people thinking I am quacko just because I was friendly to Nathan Hunderchunk, who I do not even know.

So I think I will stay away from him, as much as I can.

o   o   o   o   o   o   o   o   o

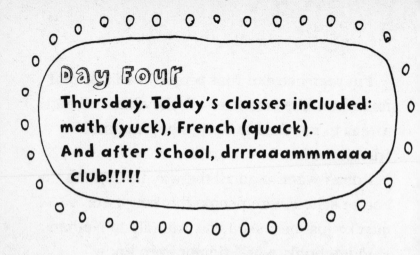

Day Four

Thursday. Today's classes included:
math (yuck), French (quack).
And after school, drrraaammmaaa
club!!!!!

We had our first drama club meeting today.
Oooh, Diary, it was so exciting actually
STANDING on the very stage where I first saw
Keisha acting A Little Princess!

Me and Keisha got to the auditorium early,
and our footsteps echoed importantly and
nervously as we went down toward the stage. I
kept imagining that the auditorium was FULL of
people, who had all come to see me and Keisha
act...

"I'll show you how to get onto the stage from
the wings," said Keisha excitedly. "Look, there's
this door here, and it goes around the back—"

But just then the door opened and Mr. Trucillo, the drama teacher, came out. And guess what? He is the one with the blue Mohawk!

He smiled at us, and said, "Time for that later, girls!" Then he looked at me. "Are you the new one?"

I nodded, and I said in a rush, "But I've done lots of acting before...I mean, in my bedroom..."

"Well, I know you'll enjoy drama club. We're a friendly bunch here, and we'll make sure you don't feel too nervous onstage."

Onstage!!!

Ooh, dear Diary, I was SO excited! My first step on the road to Movie-Star-dom!

I was slightly out-Movie-Starred by Alicia, though. She Sashayed into the auditorium, talking loudly to her Angels about how much she was looking forward to being in the play.

Sashaying is a very Movie-Star walk – you

put your chin in the air and swing your hips around wildly and bang through doors without looking who is on the other side of them. It's particularly good if you can manage to toss your hair at the same time. I was a little envious that I had not thought of Sashaying myself, but I was too busy Trotting. This is a very good walk for school, because it makes you look confident and eager, which teachers like; also it gets you past Hannah Lumb quickly. It is a little like doing that pretend pony thing you did when you were five, only without the reins.

Nathan is also in drama club! He does the lights, which means he has a lot of power. He can bathe you in glory or plunge you into darkness. It also means he doesn't have to talk to anyone or be onstage and he seems to like that. I was surprised to see him there, after what Alicia said. Being in drama club seems a very uh-quacko thing to do. But maybe

he hides his quacko-ness under a bushel?
I mean, maybe he is quacko inside and it
doesn't show?

Mr. Trucillo turned out to be really nice.
He is really clear about what you have to do
(not like some teachers!) and he makes you
feel good and as if you can do things well.
And he behaves as if he likes us (again not
like some teachers!!).

He is also extraordinarily bendy, as I found
out when we had to do warm-up exercises
(not on the stage, but in the auditorium).
Keisha says he used to be a dancer and that's
why. The only non-bendy part of him is his
blue Mohawk. (I wonder how he sleeps in it?)

After the warm-up we did some
improvisation (still not on the stage, just in
the auditorium) and then we talked about the
play we're going to do this year. It is a
comedy – hooray! It has a Greek name,
Pygmalion, though I don't know why because

it is set in London. It is about a poor flower-selling girl named Eliza, who gets turned into a princess, as far as I can gather. BUT! The even more important thing is that we talked about the Dramarama Camp Application.

The application has to be emailed in a month's time. It is a computer folder full of photos and videos of us all acting, and pieces we've written about acting too, and our own Supporting Statements which say why we want to go to Dramarama camp, and then secret reports that Mr. Trucillo writes about us to say why we should go.

"Hands up if you're going to apply to Dramarama camp this year," said Mr. Trucillo.

I stuck my hand up really high, and so did Keisha, and so did nine other people including Alicia, but not Nathan.

"This year," said Mr. Trucillo, "everything has to be done online! Thankfully we've got the excellent new school computers – any of you who are in school newspaper club or have had IT have probably already used them. Nathan is going to help by making videos of you acting, using the school digital camera, and those can be part of the application. Thank you, Nathan, for volunteering! Any questions?"

"Will we have to write a new Supporting Statement this year?" asked one of the girls.

"Will it make a difference that I wasn't in last year's play?" asked a boy. "I did the props, does that count?"

Then they all started talking. Especially Alicia. Dear Diary, everyone seems to know exactly what they're doing, as if they went to Dramarama camp all the time! They already have lots of pictures and clips of them acting in the play they did last year. And I bet they are really good. And I don't have anything yet.

Another worrying thing is this play needs a cockney accent. Which I have no idea how to do. It sounds like athletics for the mouth!

Mr. Trucillo saw that I was looking really worried. He leaned over and said, "The application isn't all about how much acting you've done, Bathsheba. It's a lot about your Supporting Statement, too." And then he smiled at me really kindly, and said, "And after all, if you don't get selected for this summer, there's always next year."

He is really kind and nice, so I tried to smile back.

But oh, dear Diary, I really, really want to go THIS year!

Next year is too late. Anything could have happened by next year. I can't even imagine next year. I will be in Eighth Grade, which will be extraordinary.

Anyway, I knew there was no point in moping, so I tried to Think Positive and make the most of drama club, because I thought even if I don't get into Dramarama camp, I could still be a famous actress later on in life.

And then finally – FINALLY – Mr. Trucillo said, "Let's show Bathsheba some of the acting techniques we've learned, shall we? Bath, why don't you hop up on the stage?"

"Ooh," I said. Because I have never really stood on a real stage before, dear Diary. My bed does not count.

I went up the steps to the stage very carefully, trying to feel as much like a Movie Star as possible. I tried to swoosh, as if I was not wearing a school uniform, but a glittering Red Carpet dress.

I walked right out into the center of the stage, and I turned, and looked at my audience.

Dear Diary, it is a lot further up and lonelier on the stage than I ever imagined.

I looked down at everyone, sitting on the floor, or on chairs, and Mr. Trucillo with his blue Mohawk in the middle, and they were all looking at me. As if they expected me to...act.

Chanelle giggled. I swallowed. All of a sudden, the auditorium felt very big, and I felt very small. I could feel my knees getting uncertain of themselves.

"To be or not to be," I squeaked, because that is the kind of thing actors say.

Everyone laughed, dear Diary! I could feel myself going hot and cold. I tried to smile. Were they laughing at me? I wondered. In a horrible way? Keisha was smiling, but I was feeling so panicky I could hardly see her.

"You just need to stand there for a moment, Bathsheba," said Mr. Trucillo. "Just get a sense of the space around you."

I tried to stop myself from fleeing into the wings. They looked shadowy and inviting. I took a deep breath, and told myself, I am Bathsheba Clarice de Trop! I am FANTASTIC!

It almost worked.

"Anyone got any ideas about how Bath could feel more comfortable up there?"

Keisha's hand shot up.

"Okay, Keisha, go ahead."

"Bath!" Keisha said. "Just count the number of floor tiles."

"Eek?"

"Just count them."

I managed to take my mind off how BIG the auditorium was, and how lonely I felt. I started counting the floor tiles. There are a LOT of them, dear Diary. It was really hard keeping my place. I forgot all about being onstage.

"...thirty-one, thirty-two, thirty-three..."

I looked up in surprise, because everyone was clapping and laughing. I smiled back at them, suddenly feeling completely comfortable.

"You see, Bath," said Mr. Trucillo, "it's just a little exercise we do with everyone who's new, to show them how easy it is to get over stage fright. It might feel scary being up on a stage in front of people, but actually, as soon as you have something else to do – like counting floor tiles, or remembering lines – you realize that it's not that scary after all. Great job! You can get down now."

Huh, dear Diary, stage fright – as if! I was just a little nervous...that's all.

o   o   o   o   o   o   o   o   o

Day Five

Friday. After school, sitting in the kitchen, watching next door's fat cat walking along the fence — oops, it fell off.

Alicia really likes me, dear Diary! Everyone is jealous!

Today she came to school with a huge red folder full of newspaper and magazine cuttings. She opened it up really excitedly and pointed to a picture. "Look!" she said. "This is so cool!"

Aargh, dear Diary, it was a picture of me and Mother coming out of the theater. I remember that photo being taken – we were just behind Madonna, who was the person all the paparazzi were actually aiming for, and because Mother can look a little like Madonna in a bad light, they took a photo of us too in the confusion. I was wearing a pink fairy outfit complete with wand. (I was younger then!!!)

The caption read, *Bestselling author Mandy de Trop and her daughter, Bathsheba Clarice, at the launch of Madonna's latest children's book.*

Alicia was just glowing. She squeezed my hand in front of everyone. "I can't believe I'm friends with someone who's been in a magazine!"

And then she said, "I'm going to sit next to you in all our classes, Bathsheba!"

Chanelle and Davina looked a little worried, because they usually sit next to her (one on each side).

I opened my mouth to protest that Keisha always sits next to me, but Alicia was looking at me as if I was a real Movie Star already. "You are *soooo* lucky," she sighed. "I bet you go in limousines all the time, and people recognize you wherever you go, and you always get special VIP entrance to stores and stuff, and designers send you presents."

Actually sometimes Mother does get sent free books by publishers, so I sort of inflated myself a little and said, "Well, yes, it is rather good being me! My life has been terribly glamorous up to date!! Being recognized on a daily basis is a trial, of course, but you learn to live with fame."

"Oh, Bath," said Keisha very grumpily, "stop showing off!"

Alicia said, "Ooh, think it just got chilly in here. Why don't we move on, Angels. See you later, Bath."

After she had gone, I said to Keisha, "You don't like her, do you?"

"Who?"

"Come on, Keisha, it's really obvious!" I was feeling miffed that she had made Alicia feel so unwelcome. And been so grumpy to me! (Even though I did probably deserve it.)

"I mean, I think you should be glad that I'm making friends!"

"I am! Of course! But—"

"But what?"

She looked a little embarrassed and wiggly, and then she said "Look, Bath – Alicia is two-faced. She makes all sorts of trouble."

I said, "But everyone else likes her."

"Huh, not really! They just don't want to get on her bad side."

"What do you mean? What does she do?"

"Well, that's the thing, she never does *anything* herself. She gets other people to do mean stuff for her. She's sly!"

Dear Diary, I was really shocked to hear Keisha say that. She normally never says anything bad about anyone! And also, it was not a very nice thing to hear, because I had been feeling quite proud, dear Diary, of being chosen to be super-popular Alicia's friend.

"Like what?" I asked. "What did she do?"

But Keisha just went all huffy, and said, "I can't explain, because it's a secret I promised never to tell, but she did something really mean last year! Don't be friends with her – you'll regret it!"

A secret?

Dear Diary, I thought best friends weren't supposed to have secrets from each other. I felt a little...worried.

I said, "I'm not asking, I'm just commenting, Keisha, but I thought you couldn't have secrets from a best friend?"

Keisha looked embarrassed. "*Please* don't ask me, Bath. I promised someone before I even met you that I would never tell anyone about it." And then she turned red and hid behind a book.

"What someone?" I asked, feeling even more worried inside.

"I can't tell you that either," she mumbled, and then the bell rang and we had to go to math.

After petting the cat next door for a while (our neighbor, Mrs. Brodie, says his name is Seamus).

Dear Diary,
I can't stop thinking about the secret. And feeling... well...a little hurt. It is no good being open and loving to a friend, and sort of rushing to them with your

arms wide open, if they then plonk a great big stony SECRET in front of you so you bash into it painfully. (If you see what I mean, DD.)

And I also keep worrying about this person. This other friend, who I don't know about. Who she likes so much that she's prepared to keep a secret from me for them.

And yet...I know Keisha wouldn't lie to me,

so I suppose I should try and keep out of Alicia's way in the future. But it is a pity! I was looking forward to her being my second-best friend. And she really does seem to like me! *Sigh*.

But I know Keisha really IS the most wonderful friend in the world. This first week could have been so bad, and it is all because of her that going to school was not that awful (at least, not mostly) and actually was splendacious! She should be allowed one secret. I bet she will tell me soon anyway...

Maybe I should make Keisha a knighthood or something. To show her what good friends we are. I could cut a star out of paper and cover it with silver foil and write on it "MEDAL FOR A GREAT FRIEND." Or maybe a better word than great. Like super...supercilious.

After dinner (shepherd's pie! It collapsed a little, but it was * still yummy). 6

What a good thing I have Bill to help me with things like making Friend Medals! He gave me really good advice about making decorations for them, using tinsel, and the chain piece off an old bath plug. It was very kind of him, especially as he would obviously rather have been watching *Football Round-Up*. Mother would never have even let me make a Friend Medal in the living room, in case of glue on the furniture.

And also, he told me that supercilious does not mean what I meant it to at all! It means snobby. Whoops! So it is going to be a medal for a megabulous friend instead.

Wow, I am glad the first week of school is over, though! I have been *sooooo* busy! It's nice to have time just to relax and do fun things like make Friend Medals.

o   o   o   o   o   o   o   o   o

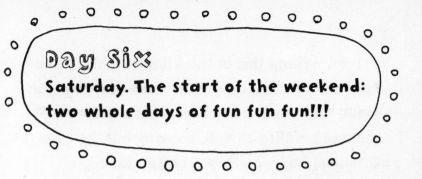

Day Six

Saturday. The start of the weekend: two whole days of fun fun fun!!!

It's the weekend, dear Diary!!!! Wake up and smell the...uh, Rice Crispies is I think what we are having for breakfast. Which don't really smell, so never mind.

Anyway! Wooo!!! I have a whole two days = forty-eight hours = millions of minutes = gazillion squillions of seconds (you do the math, dear Diary, I don't have to because I am not at school!) to do Anything I Like in!!

Happy happy. Weekendy.

I've never had a weekend before, dear Diary. Well, of course they were there really, but unless you are going to school (or work, I suppose) every other day of the week, you don't really notice them come and go.

I am writing this at the kitchen table. After I got up, I trotted down the stairs and over the piano and into the kitchen, where Bill was making breakfast (well, pouring out the Rice Crispies) and whistling a chirpy tune.

"Are you looking for a job again today?" I asked.

"Oh, yes. You never know what may turn up overnight. I've got the papers to go through – and I'll pop over to the library to use the printer, seeing as ours is busted again."

"Oh, I bet you'll find a job really quickly," I said happily. "I mean, you're trying so hard, you must!"

"Well, that's the idea, anyway! I'm not picky – and I'm a lot more qualified than most of the people at the job center."

"You are Spectacular," I told him. "You could borrow one of my feather boas, if you like. They boost my confidence, anyway."

Bill laughed, which was nice. I like to be entertaining. I have not forgotten about Keisha saying I would make a great comedy actress, Diary. She said that right when she first met me, and I was giving her a tour of the Palatial Mansion I used to live in. I saw her in last year's school play, and she's such a good actress herself that she must know what she's talking about.

So anyway, today me and Keisha are going to get *Pygmalion* out of the library and we're going to read it and then have a sleepover in my space pod so we can practice our lines! I can't wait for my first EVER sleepover with a best friend! Ooh, dear Diary, I've made sure everything is going to be perfect. I've put my new, Princesscular bedspread on the spare mattress (it only JUST fits – my whole bedroom floor is mattress now!) for Keisha, and I've got some delicious hot chocolate for just before bed, and also books on acting from the library. I have also got some CDs, but only very quiet music that you don't have to really listen to, because this is an acting sleepover, and not just a fun one. We will be acting and reading out parts of *Pygmalion*, all night long, I think!

And, dear Diary – I have a secret plan. All I can tell you is that it involves the words *Keisha*, and *Secret*, and *Truth or Dare* and *Bathsheba* (as in, me) *Getting Told Keisha's Secret Because We Are Best Friends*!

You see, I bet Keisha wants to tell me her secret really. She just needs some prompting!

Afternoon. Back from town!

I have just been to the library, with Keisha and Bev and Bill. Keisha went on the computers and googled basketball players, for the *Clotborough School Gazette*, I suppose.

I signed all Mother's books that were in the children's section. I would think the librarians will be delighted with that – I have probably made them worth thousands. Now they can sell them on eBay and buy more computers, which will be good, because we had to wait in line to use the ones they've got.

I do not like to be thanked for these little acts of kindness, Diary, it is enough to have a Nice Warm Glow inside. Oatmeal has the same effect, so on days I eat oatmeal I won't bother with little acts of kindness.

Alicia was at the library too, in the Reference section, where I hardly ever go because the books smell of math. She was sitting at a table with a frowny man who I guessed was her dad. He was reading a HUGE book with an equation on the front of it. I would be frowny too, if I had to read that!

Alicia waved and gave me a secret smile when she saw me. I waved back – and then felt guilty because of Keisha (who didn't see Alicia because she was too busy learning about basketball. Hmm, actually I've just remembered that Keisha's doing an article on global warming for the *Gazette* at the moment, so the basketball stuff can't have been for that. I wonder what it was for then? Weird).

Oh dear Diary, I am sure that tonight Keisha will relent and tell me the secret. She can't keep it from me forever. Not if she is really my best friend. She probably just has to explain things to the other person and say, "Look, I know I said I wouldn't tell anyone, but I have a best friend now, and things are different, so please can I tell her…?"

I bet the person would let her tell me, if she asked like that.

Later afternoon... *☆
almost evening...

Dear Diary,
Me and Keisha are both so disappointed
with *Pygmalion*!

I mean, it started out good. There was a
funny scene with flower-sellers, and Eliza
(who's the heroine) being a Drama Queen
and shrieking and going, "Aah-ow-ooh!" a lot,
which is "Oh!" but in a cockney accent. She
was all upset because she thought Professor
Higgins (who's sort of the hero) was a
detective and was going to get her in trouble,
but in fact he was just being incredibly clever
by knowing everything about people, like what
school they went to, just from their accent.

But then Keisha said (because she reads
faster than me), "Actually, Professor Higgins
is horrible! He just called Eliza a squashed
cabbage leaf!"

"Oh, that's okay. It's a romantic play. They'll end up in love if they're arguing," I told her.

But they don't! (I skipped to the end, which I know is cheating, but I needed to know!)

What happens is, Professor Higgins (who is really bossy and annoying!) says he will turn Eliza into a lady and teach her to speak in a fancy accent, because he thinks her own is horrible.

Well, instead of saying, "Bug off, I would rather sell flowers" – or flaʌrs, which is what it sounds like in her accent – "than have you being supercilious, which means snobby, about my accent," she goes along with him. I can sort of understand why, because she has no money or anything, so what else was she supposed to do? She does really well at acting fancy, and at a special ball everyone thinks she is a princess. But the Professor just doesn't appreciate her at all, he is just really pleased with himself and doesn't pay any attention to her, so of course she feels lonely and upset.

And then the Professor, who is supposed to be the hero, refuses to fall in love with her like he should! So Eliza obviously can't marry him, so she marries a boy named Freddy instead, which is NONSENSE because everyone knows that it is the one that the heroine has all the arguments with that she should end up marrying!

Honestly, I think Mr. George Bernard Shaw who wrote it should watch a few romantic comedies before trying to write one, because this *Pygmalion* is completely wrong.

Me and Keisha practiced some lines from the play anyway. Eliza is definitely the best character, she is such a Drama Queen! She has to say, "I'm a goo-ood girl, I am!" and, "Garn!" and, "Aah-oow-ooow!" She has to flounce around and shriek. I can do that! Easily!!

But it ought to have a happy ending, dear Diary. Why couldn't Mr. Trucillo find us a play with some nice costumes and a love story and...and songs? Huh.

Really late at night. Keisha is asleep.

Dear Diary,
I am sorry if I have woken you up. But I am miserable, and I have to tell someone about it – and I can't tell Keisha because the misery is sort of her fault!

You know I mentioned I had a plan? With the words *Keisha*, and *Bathsheba*, and *Secret*, and *Truth or Dare* in it?

Well, it failed. And now Keisha's upset with me.

I thought I planned it really well. After we'd done so much acting that we couldn't do anymore – and talked about what we'd do if we were famous Movie Stars and getting chased by photographers all the time – and what we'd wear to the Oscars – and if we'd be allowed to still have sleepovers, or was that not really Movie-Starry – I said, "Hey, I know, let's play Truth or Dare!"

Keisha said "Okay!" So we played a few rounds. I did a Dare of doing an impression of Miss Kinsey (which made Keisha laugh so hard that Bill came in to see if we were okay), and Keisha did a Truth of "Which do you really like more – school newspaper club, or drama club?" (She said school newspaper club!) And I did a Truth of "If you had to choose between your mother and your father forever, which one would you choose?" (That was HARD, dear Diary! Actually, I told Keisha I couldn't say, and she was really nice and said that was okay, she couldn't either, and I didn't have to do a Dare because it wasn't a fair question.)

And then, dear Diary, I put my plan into action!

The next time Keisha chose a Truth, I took a deep breath.

"Truth: 'What's the secret about Alicia?'" I asked.

"I can't tell you that! I'll do a Dare instead."

"No, wait!" I said. "Then who's the someone whose secret it is?"

"I can't tell you, Bath! I already said that about a million times! It's a really, really big secret and I promised never to tell anyone." She was looking upset, but also pretty angry. And then she said, "Did you just want to play Truth or Dare so you could trick me into telling my secret, Bath? I bet you did!"

"No! No! I mean...yes," I said, feeling really upset and also guilty and also annoyed.

"Oh, Bath!" she said furiously. And then she flumped down on the spare mattress and said, "I'm going to sleep!" But not in a yawn-I'm-going-to-sleep way. More in a I'm-really-upset-and-going-to-lie-here-not-looking-at-you-while-you-try-to-apologize sort of way.

So I apologized and apologized, and in the end she forgave me, and now she really is asleep, but dear Diary, I am not happy. I am dying to know what this huge secret is! It's horrible!! Knowing there is a secret you can never ever be told is like having a Christmas present you can never ever unwrap! Horrible, horrible, horrible!! And this is my BEST FRIEND giving me this un-unwrappable present (if you see what I mean, DD).

Oh, I wish I had never heard of this secret. It feels as if it is spoiling *everything*.

o   o   o   o   o   o   o   o   o

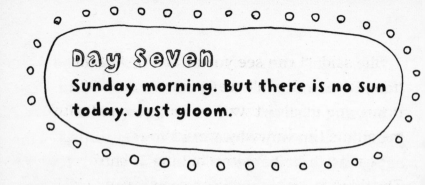

Day Seven

Sunday morning. But there is no sun today. Just gloom.

Bad, sad news, dear Diary.

Even though the Truth or Dare moment was horrible, I really did have lots of fun practicing lines and stuff with Keisha yesterday, and I thought we could meet up next Saturday too, to rehearse some more.

But Keisha is going to be busy next Saturday. And all the following Saturday mornings. She is going to cheerleading practice and trying out for the squad; she told me over breakfast. I wondered if it was because she was still upset with me from last night, and the stupid secret. But I didn't ask, in case it was, since then I would just have felt worse.

She said, "I can see you all the rest of the time, Bath, it doesn't really matter, does it? I mean, you wouldn't want to hang around with me all the time anyway, would you?"

I tried to Think Positive but it was hard. The thing is, I have not been seeing as much of Keisha as I had hoped I would. She is always busy outside school. We are in school newspaper club together, and drama club, but she seems to have something on every single evening now that school has started. I do wonder how she manages to do her homework.

"Well, I bet cheerleading will be fun!" I said. And then I said, "Maybe I could try out for the squad, too!"

"Um," said Keisha. And then there was a horrible gap in the conversation, about the same size as the gap between me and Mother when we are talking to each other on the phone, except this gap was not distance across the sea, it was something else.

"Well," I said. "Okay. Nevermind."

And soon after, Keisha went home.

Sunday afternoon. And now it is raining.

I do not really feel like going on with making the Friendship Medal for Keisha anymore.
I feel angry and upset. Maybe it's not fair to, but I do. Why didn't she want me to go to cheerleading with her? I'm her best friend!

And what about this horrible secret?

Who can Keisha like so much that she's prepared to keep their secret, even though it means upsetting her best friend??

I hope I really *am* Keisha's best friend!!!

I just called Keisha in a panic. "Am I really your best friend?"

"Of course you are, Bath! Duh!" she said.

"Oh, okay," I said, feeling really relieved, because she did sound like she meant it.

Midnight.

Ugh. Was just woken up by someone shouting in the scary house. I peered out of the window and a man who looked like a pit bull came out of the front door and slammed it behind him.

He looked really grumpy. Not at all like our nice neighbors on either side.

Eek, dear Diary! He looked up at my window!

I hid really quickly. I hope he didn't see me staring at him...

o   o   o   o   o   o   o   o   o

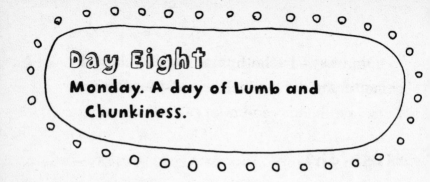

Day Eight
Monday. A day of Lumb and Chunkiness.

More eek, dear Diary!

Today Hannah Lumb got me and Keisha in a corner of the cafeteria and said, "So you're the girl whose mother writes all those stupid books?"

I said, "They're not stupid!"

"Ha! Yeah, as if things ever happen the way they do in books. Like, the thieves getting caught in *Bathsheba's Paris Plot*, or in *Bathsheba's Pony Crisis*, when the pony from the rescue center ended up winning the prize, or when you saved the president from man-eating wolves in *Bathsheba and the Time Machine*, or when..."

I looked at Keisha and Keisha looked at

me, and we were both thinking the same thing, dear Diary, which was, *Wow, Hannah Lumb really has read a lot of Bathsheba books!*

BUT, we were far too smart to actually say that to her, dear Diary. Instead, Keisha had a brainwave, which was to say really loudly, "Oh, Miss Kinsey, HELP!"

Hannah jumped and as she was looking around nervously for Miss Kinsey (who wasn't there) me and Keisha RAN in the opposite direction. Miss Kinsey is the only teacher Hannah is afraid of. She confuses her with big words.

But then guess what?

Nathan Hunderchunk passed me a note in science. I was worried it was going to be something scary, like the circuit board, but do you know what it said?

DEAR BATHSHEBA

I THINK HANNAH LUMB IS STUPID.
I AM A BIG FAN OF ALL YOUR BOOKS!
MY FAVORITE IS THE PARIS PLOT,
WHERE YOU STEAL BACK THE
STOLES THE STEALERS STOLE.

NATHAN HUNDERCHUNK.

(*Bathsheba's Paris Plot* is one of Mother's bestselling books. In it, an evil dress designer steals some really expensive stoles, which are like fancy scarves, from her rival. Bathsheba finds out who did it, and she steals them back again, which is really smart because the evil designer can't go to the police because she stole the stoles in the first place!)

Anyway, it was really nice to read that note. It gave me a warm feeling inside. I started thinking how Nathan was maybe not so quacko after all. I smiled at him across the classroom, but I don't think he saw – he was reading very hard and his ears were pink.

And then I opened my bag to get my pencil case, and I SHRIEKED because there was something with wires sticking out of it and lights blinking on it in there!!!

Mr. Runcibald made me take it up to the front. He looked at it and said, "Well, it's a very *good* homemade kitchen timer, Bathsheba, but I don't think you should be playing with it in science."

So now all the class thinks I am quacko enough to make homemade kitchen timers and play with them in class, and it is so obviously Nathan Hunderchunk's fault!

No one else would put something like that in my bag!

OOH, dear Diary, I am really angry with him for getting me into trouble.

o   o   o   o   o   o   o   o   o

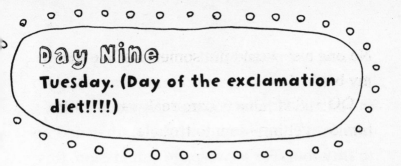

Day Nine
Tuesday. (Day of the exclamation diet!!!!)

Miss Kinsey has put me on an exclamation mark diet!!! (Which I just sort of forgot about, oops.)

She called me up to the front during the English lesson and said, "Bathsheba, about the essay you did for homework..."

"'What I Did On My Summer Break'," I said, nodding. "I know it sounds made-up, but it's honestly all true, especially the parts about chips and beans."

"Oh, I believe you. But you didn't actually write an essay entitled 'What I Did On My Summer Break', did you, Bathsheba?"

"I did!" I said indignantly.

"No, what you in fact wrote was 'What I Did On My Summer Break!!!!!!!!'" She shuffled around her papers and pulled out my essay. Every single exclamation mark was circled in red ink. "I have counted the exclamation marks in your essay; Bathsheba, they add up to fifty-four. For a two-page submission, this seems excessive."

"It was a very exciting break!"

"I am not sure that anyone's summer can be exciting enough to justify fifty-four exclamation marks, not even James Bond's. From now on, I am placing you on a diet."

I squidged my stomach worriedly. Mother does keep writing anxious e-mails about how I should make sure not to put on weight while she is away, but I thought I was okay.

"A punctuation diet. No more exclamation marks! If you feel you absolutely must use one, you should write an explanation of why you use it, and hand that in to me along with your essay."

I opened and closed my mouth in horror.

"But I'll end up having to write twice as much!"

"You see my cunning plan," agreed Miss Kinsey.

"But – but if I don't use exclamation marks, everything I write will be so boring!"

Miss Kinsey tapped her pen on the desk impatiently.

"Then you will have to find other ways of conveying your enthusiasm. How about broadening your vocabulary?"

"I don't think I have one," I said.

"A vocabulary is the number of words you know, and let me assure you that every pupil in my class is expected to have one." She looked at me over her glasses. "Punctuation is not a right, Bathsheba, it is a privilege."

And then she gave me this huge book, which is called a word that sounds like a dinosaur – let me see – oh yes, THESAURUS. With which I am supposed to broaden my vocabulary. Possibly by flattening it under the book.

It is actually really interesting. I did not know there were so many words in the world – it is enough to make one feel JADED. Which means tired and fed up. According to this dinosaur-sized book.

I moaned and moaned to Keisha about my punctuation diet at break time, but she seemed distracted. I think it was because the boys were playing basketball really close to where we were trying to talk, and making a lot of noise. Rafiq was playing too. Not very well – he kept knocking the ball over toward us and Keisha had to keep getting up to give it back to him. I don't think he can be all that good at basketball after all, or he'd keep the ball on the field or whatever it's called, instead of getting in the way of my and Keisha's conversation. Huh! I said so to Keisha.

"He IS good at basketball!" she said grumpily, and it seemed as if she was going to say something else, but then she decided not to. Anyway the next time he knocked the ball over to us she didn't go and get it for him.

Nathan was sort of shuffling around the edges of the game as if he wanted to play but didn't dare to ask. I felt sorry for him, but it was a squirmy kind of sorry, dear Diary. I feel as if I ought to try and be friends with him, because no one else is, and he was nice about my books. But he is quacko and his brother sounds scary and...well, I don't want to!

And now I feel mean.

School newspaper club was really good, though! I got to be a Roving Reporter, and go around school looking for people to interview. As it was after school there weren't many people around, so I ended up interviewing Rafiq, who was there for extra basketball practice. I asked him about being a Basketball Star, but all he said was "Yeah," and "No," and "I dunno". Honestly. How am I supposed to turn that into a thrilling article?

Alicia was Roving too, and somehow we ended up Roving together, because Keisha was busy helping Miss Kinsey with layout things (Miss Kinsey still doesn't like the computers). Alicia told me all kinds of incredible things about the Ninth and Tenth Graders and even the teachers. I know newspapers are not supposed to be full of gossip, but it IS interesting! I had no idea that Mr. Runcibald has three false teeth in the middle! I will have to look very carefully during science class.

And then she wanted to know all about me, and Mother, and the Palatial Mansion. And by the time we got back to the computer room, somehow we were walking along arm in arm, as if we were best friends or something. When we walked in like that, Keisha gave me this funny look, and I thought *Oops!* and had to let go hurriedly and slink into my seat and ignore Alicia for the rest of the class. Which didn't feel polite, but what else could I do, dear Diary?

On the way home after school newspaper club I asked Keisha to show me her cheerleading moves, but she said she isn't very good yet. I don't know when the tryouts for the squad are. She changes the subject every time I try and ask her.

I couldn't help thinking, dear Diary, that it's funny how Alicia isn't my best friend, but she tells me everything. And Keisha is my best friend...but she doesn't tell me everything. At all.

o   o   o   o   o   o   o   o   o

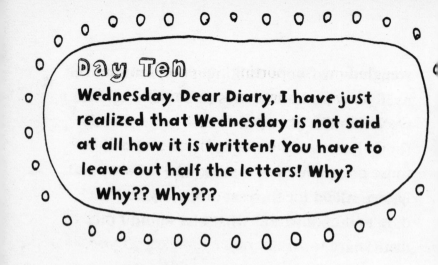

Day Ten

Wednesday. Dear Diary, I have just realized that Wednesday is not said at all how it is written! You have to leave out half the letters! Why? Why?? Why???

Miss Kinsey caught me writing my Dramarama Supporting Statement under the desk in English today! She said "SEE ME AFTER CLASS." I was so scared!

"Will I get expelled?" I asked Keisha. I was nearly crying, dear Diary!

"No, of course not, Bath! She'll just be a little stern, probably. Go on – I'll wait for you outside."

When I went up to her desk, Miss Kinsey looked at me over her glasses, and then she said, "What exactly is this document?" and waggled my Supporting Statement at me.

"It's my Dramarama Supporting Statement," I whimpered.

"Oh yes, of course. Mr. Trucillo mentioned these to me. Writing it in my class, however, is not a good idea." She turned my paper over and over, and then she said, "You really want to go to Dramarama camp, don't you, young lady?"

I nodded silently, feeling full of terror, because it is never good when someone calls you a "young lady," dear Diary.

"Hmm. Well, I suggest that to begin with, you improve your Supporting Statement. You can do much, much better than this effort, I am sure."

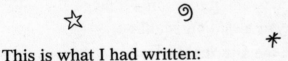

This is what I had written:

Dear Dramarama camp!!!
I am so dying to come and be part of the whole Dramarama thing!! I already have your stickers that I have put on my shoes. I want to come because my friend Keisha is coming and also because I want to be a star!!! Actually, I already am a star, so I know you will be really pleased to have me there. I have my own feather boa and everything. Plus my mother has friends in Hollywood. Oh, please let me come!!! I am very loud and bouncy and have millions of friends, also I am very dramatic already so you won't have to teach me anything.

So please please please please please can I come?????

Thank you a million squillion,
Bathsheba Clarice de Trop

Miss Kinsey read it again, and then she turned it upside down and read it, and then she sighed and shook her head and said, "No, it's no better like that."

I could feel tears coming into my eyes. Miss Kinsey patted me on the head. She meant it kindly, but I have no idea why anyone would think that was cheering. Tap tap tap. I felt like a basketball.

"You see, Bathsheba," she explained, "you have to show them that you are responsible and mature, and that you can work as part of a team as well as show off."

"I'm not a show-off!!!"

"No, I know that, but your letter does come across as rather...bumptious."

(BUMPTIOUS. What a good word. I have a feeling I will like to be bumptious, whatever that turns out to be.)

**(Having looked in the ♭
dictionary.)** ☆

Huh!! I am *not* bumptious!

Anyway, Miss Kinsey sighed, and said, "You
are off the deep end, aren't you? New school,
new house, new parent. Bathsheba,
I will help you with this Supporting
Statement, because once I was a little girl,
just like you."

I blinked at her. I cannot imagine her ever
having been *just* like me, dear Diary.

"Yes," she added, "once I too had dreams
of the stage. They came to nothing. Real Life
ground them under its heel. But yours may
still flourish, and I think working on this
Supporting Statement will also improve your
writing skills. We will tackle it together, in
spare moments at school newspaper club."

Wow, dear Diary! How nice of her!

She patted me on the head again, but this time I didn't mind at all.

*

Later...

6

Dear Diary,
HORRORS!!!

Nathan Hunderchunk has just left the scary house opposite (rather suddenly, as if he was thrown out – oh dear). He is now Mooching across the grass. I hope he can't see me watching him.

I may not be just like the Bathsheba in the books, but I can figure out a few detective clues when I have to...

This means, dear Diary, that Nathan Hunderchunk lives right across from me!!!

In the scary house!!!

And the pit-bull person I keep seeing walking his horrible dogs around and

shouting nasty things must be his brother,
Jason! Of Gym Attempted Conflagration
(thesaurus: burning up, or down) Fame!
   Oh NO!!!

O   O   O   O   O   O   O   O   O   O

Day Eleven

Thursday. Ooh, Bill says that days are named after ancient gods. And Thursday is the day of Thor, god of thunder.
No sign of thunder today, though...

Today in drama club we started practicing scenes from *Pygmalion*. Me and Keisha complained about the play not having a happy ending. Mr. Trucillo just said, "Well, I think it's time we tackled some larger themes, don't you, girls?"

"We could have larger themes and still a happy ending," I said hopefully. But he just laughed.

We tried doing a scene where Eliza's dad comes to see her, and we find out that actually he's abandoned Eliza and just wants to get money out of her. Everyone was laughing, because Eliza's dad is really funny, but I couldn't help thinking of the bad old days when Bill had abandoned me (I thought), and I felt sad for Eliza, too.

We also found out that the auditions are next week! So I have to decide what part I want to try out for. Eliza is the only part I really want to play...but everyone says Alicia is bound to get that so maybe I should try for another part. Alicia is really good at her cockney accent. She even did it when we were doing improvisations, which was a little silly as we were supposed to be pretending to be trees. Mr. Trucillo looked a little annoyed at how much his forest (us) was talking. He said, "Alicia, you don't have the part yet, you know. Give it a rest."

I was a copper beech. I concentrated on Tree Thoughts, like Growing Leaves and Not Getting Turned Into IKEA Furniture. It was calming. I walked around leafily for the rest of the day.

I got an e-mail from my mother!

From: BuyBathshebaBooksToday
To: MeMeMeMeMeMe!!
Subject: From Your Loving Mother

Dear Bathsheba,
How are you? I hope you have not caught any terrible diseases from that horrible neighborhood. Your father was never much good at keeping the house clean. I don't suppose he has changed. Hollywood is still wonderful. I am making lots of connections and my appointments book is full for weeks to come. I know this Bathsheba movie will be a hit. If only you could be here at St. Agnes' Stage School with Avocado; it would be a great opportunity for you.

I do miss you, darling. Remember, you can come and stay during school breaks. I will arrange new teeth for you – just say the word and I will send the catalog.

Affectionately yours,
Mandy

New teeth???

What sort of new teeth???

Dear Diary,
Sigh. I do sometimes wish I were in
Hollywood. There would be palm trees.
Imagine waking up and seeing palm trees!!!
Here, I wake up and see Bill's second-best
alarm clock. It has Mickey Mouse on it, and
his arms go around and around in ways I am
sure a mouse's arms cannot possibly go
without breaking.

Bill is downstairs being really busy writing job
application letters yet again. I can hear him
muttering and banging the computer around.
This is the only way to make it print.

I wonder what sort of job he will get in
the end. I think he should be a DJ or a TV
presenter or something like that. But when
I suggested it to him he said, "Try to be

realistic, Bathsheba! The way things are going, I'll be lucky to get a job as a garbage man."

I wonder if he is angry with me? I feel a little DOWNCAST. Which means more or less what it says. Eliza's dad is a garbage man. But he is horrible to her. I think Bill would be nice whatever job he had.

Speaking (or writing!) of Eliza, I have decided I WILL audition for her. I am practicing my cockney accent all the time, even at school. I think it is the hardest thing I've ever done! My mouth just doesn't go like that naturally.

o   o   o   o   o   o   o   o   o

Day Twelve
Friday. Day of Fryer, goddess of chips...um...I think.

Alicia walked some of the way home with me this evening. She asked me to go shopping with her tomorrow! It was really flattering. But I felt bad because she didn't say anything about asking Keisha, so I said I couldn't.

Tonight Keisha is at cake-decorating class. She is trying for her Gold Piping Standard. Alicia says Keisha is an Overachiever. Well, maybe. But she is still my best friend! Even if she does have a huge secret she won't share.

Oh, and I was practicing my cockney accent down at the store on the corner, and a complete stranger lady threw her arms

around me and said it was so good to hear a
youngster speaking Welsh the old way. Hmm,
more practice needed, I think...

o o o o o o o o o

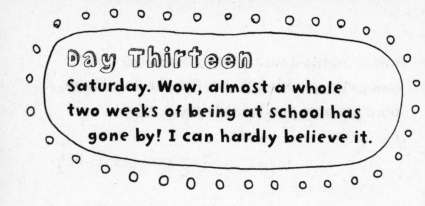

Day Thirteen

Saturday. Wow, almost a whole two weeks of being at school has gone by! I can hardly believe it.

Bored, dear Diary. Keisha is off juggling pompoms, I suppose.

Huh, now I do feel as if I would have liked to go shopping with Alicia. It would have been fun! She IS really nice to me. In class, she always tries to sit next to me whenever she can, and she always shares her magazines and even the free lipglosses and things that she gets with them.

Bill is busy with application forms. The tops of all the pens in the house look as if a mouse has been at them, except it is not a mouse, it is Bill, doing his job application forms on the dining table and chewing his pen in the meantime. If I make any noise near him he gets annoyed and says, "Bath! I am trying to concentrate!"

He has borrowed my dinosaur book to help him with the forms.

He has applied to be a baker, a waiter, a walking-stick salesman and a math teacher at Clotborough College (he says he may as well give it a try, you never know).

I must say, I didn't think it would take him this long to find a job. I thought you just go to the job center and they say, "Mr. Bill Smithee, would you like to be a lifeguard?" and you say, "Okay," and they say, "Please start tomorrow."

He is really good at Thinking Positive, though. He just says, "No one said this was going to be easy," and chews his pen a little harder.

Saturday evening.

Ooh, Mother called!

She sounded so happy. I think Hollywood is just the right place for her. She gets to go to meetings all day and hardly has to write at all. She is seeing about getting a team to write all the new Bathsheba books, and having spin-off series starring Fifi and Aurelia. There might even be a Bathsheba doll!!!

"And what about you, Bathsheba?" she asked. "Are you managing to have some fun? What did you do today?"

"Oh, I almost went shopping, but I didn't because...because I didn't have any money," I said. I didn't really want to tell her about the whole Keisha and Alicia thing. She would probably put it in a book or something. I don't know why I should mind that so much, dear Diary. I just feel sort of as if this is *my* life, not the made-up Bathsheba's.

"But, Bathsheba, I made a special bank account for you, you know that! There is no need for you to go without anything! Bill does *know* that, doesn't he? He hasn't *spent* it, has he...?"

"No!" I said furiously. "That's a horrible thing to say, Mother!"

"Well, I am sorry, darling. I'm just worried about you, that's all."

I wished Mother hadn't called then, because she went on and on at Bill on the phone about money, and I could tell he was feeling angry and upset. I don't know exactly what she said, but after Bill got off the phone he came up to my room and said, "Bath, you know you can have that bank card whenever you want, don't you? All you have to do is ask. I don't want you to go without."

Oh dear. Life is complicated.

o   o   o   o   o   o   o   o   o

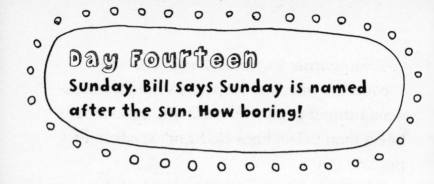

Day Fourteen

Sunday. Bill says Sunday is named after the sun. How boring!

This morning me and Bill went to IKEA with Bev and Keisha. Bill took one look at the crowds, sat down firmly in the café and said, "Why don't you text me when you're done, girls? I'll be here having a coffee." So me and Keisha and Bev walked around on our own. Me and Keisha just wanted to look at the toys (I know it's babyish, but they are so cute!) but Bev wanted to go and look at the kitchens, and then we found this amazing yellow four-poster bed which me and Keisha both SO wanted, except it had the quacko name of SPLUKKET.

But, dear Diary, all the time I was there, and all the way through eating meatballs, you know what I was thinking?

Maybe it is a little embarrassing...but I was wondering if people would think we looked like a family. You know, me and Keisha and Bill and Bev.

And I was wondering, if we really were... if I was Keisha's sister...I wonder if she would have secrets from me then?

I am trying to forget the secret, but I can't. It's as if every time I think of Keisha, a big red sign appears over her head, flashing and saying SECRET. It's horrible.

I bet if we were sisters, she'd tell me everything.

After lunch.

Keisha and me have been practicing our lines again. Keisha is going to audition for Mrs. Higgins. She is Professor Higgins's mother, and she's nice to Eliza and sorts everything out at the end. I think Keisha would be really good in that role! She's just the kind of person who sorts things out for her friends.

At least, I *think* she is. Knowing she has this secret from me is just making me wonder if I REALLY know all about Keisha the way I thought I did.

Sigh.

Anyway, we sat on the floor and I did my Eliza noises.

"Aaah-ooww-oooh..."

"Try it a little higher," said Keisha.

"Aahh-eeeooow-oooh??"

She fell over laughing, so I think it was good!

And then someone knocked at the door, and huh, it was Mrs. Brodie from the right-hand next door, and Mrs. Kapoor from the left-hand next door. They had come over to see if we were okay, because of the terrible noises.

Mrs. Brodie said, "It sounded like a wailing banshee, and that's not something you want to hear at my age, I promise you!"

So after that I practiced my "Garn!" very quietly instead. And Keisha practiced being Mrs. Higgins, Professor Higgins's mother, and being sarcastic to Professor Higgins, which was really fun as we both think he is a bossy character who is horrible to Eliza!

After Keisha has left.

Garn is such a strange word! I cannot find it in the dictionary. I did find *banshee*, though. Apparently it's a ghost that screams when people are going to die.

Garn!

Garn!

Garn!

Bill has just come up to see if I want a cough drop because my throat sounds really bad. Huh!

I snarled, "I'm a goo-ood girl, I am!" at him, and he retreated quickly.

o o o o o o o o o

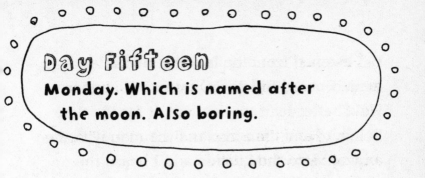

Day Fifteen

Monday. Which is named after the moon. Also boring.

Today I came home from school to find Bill and a man with an ax looking at the piano with a sort of butchery expression in their eyes.

I said, "Dad, you can't! Mother will be so angry! It's a Bechstein!"

The man said, "I thought it was a piano, hur-hur."

Bill looked embarrassed, and said, "But Bath—"

"So be it," I said tragically, "if my own father can bear to smash up with an ax the piano upon which I learned to tinkle my first tunes. Oh woe, woe! Heartless is the world!" And I Swanned off.

I listened from the landing, and after a while I heard Bill go, "Oh drat it, I suppose we'd better learn to live with it for the time being..." and then him and the man with the ax went into the kitchen and I heard them making coffee and talking about football. Ha ha! I knew it. My piano is safe!

Later...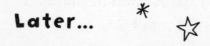

Apparently Bill met the Ax Man in prison!

He was a leading businessman in the world of Import–Export Novelties, but made bad decisions to do with taxes and a load of undeclared rubber bath ducks...

After dinner (pea and mint soup, followed by chicken casserole...Bill really likes those cookbooks of Bev's). 🫰 6

Nathan Hunderchunk just rang our doorbell! I opened it because I was closest (sitting on the piano). I am sure he was wearing exactly the same clothes as last week, and he still had his tracksuit pants tucked into his socks.

"Oh, hello," I said.

He stood there shifting from one foot to the other and opening and closing his mouth and staring at me as if I was Buckingham Palace or something. It made me feel nervous; also, I don't want anymore circuit boards, or strange blinking kitchen timers.

"I am a terribly busy person and must leave this instant," I told him, and shut the door and put the chain on.

o o o o o o o o o

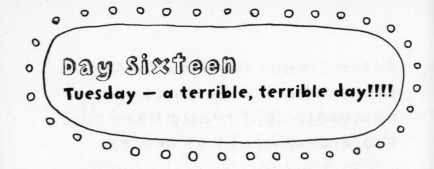

Dear Diary,

I am so upset, I don't know where to start. I've had an argument with Keisha!

I don't even really know why it happened. Oh, Diary, does this mean we are not best friends anymore? You can't argue with a best friend, can you? I thought you only argue with enemies?

Oh, does this mean Keisha is my ENEMY???

It all began going wrong at lunchtime. Nathan crept up behind me just as I was quietly eating my salad, and he pushed his earphones into my ears!

It was really loud rap music, and I was not expecting it. I sort of shrieked and leaped in the air, and shouted at Nathan and took the earphones out and threw them at him. He looked really panicky and upset while I was shouting at him and I feel bad now, but honestly, dear Diary, what was he DOING? He is completely quacko!

And I got told off by the teacher for making a scene.

But that was NOTHING to what happened in school newspaper club.

It started going wrong right from the beginning. The first annoying thing was that Keisha was working with Miss Kinsey all the time. I know Miss Kinsey is allergic to computers and Keisha keeps having to show her how to use the mouse, and Keisha does have lots of important editorial jobs which she has to do with Miss Kinsey, but it is annoying when you go to an after-school club with your friend and you can't even get to talk to her because she is always stuck with the teacher.

Also, I was trying to turn my "interview" –
huh! – with Rafiq into a thrilling article, but it
was really hard because I realized that I don't
even like basketball much. I really wished I
had chosen someone else to write about, but it
was too late and I was stuck with Rafiq. So I
was in a really grumpy mood to be honest.

Anyway, FINALLY Keisha noticed me and
came over and said hi and asked me how the
interview was going.

"Not very well," I said irritably. "Rafiq
wasn't very helpful at all! I mean, if he really
wants to be a famous sportsperson then he'll
have to do loads of interviews and stuff and
he will have to say something more
interesting than 'Yeah' and 'No' and 'I dunno'
or else he won't get any publicity because he
sounds really boring—"

"He's NOT boring!" said Keisha, only it was
more like a shout. "You just don't understand
him, Bath, he's got lots on his mind—" She

stopped quickly. I just stared at her in shock.

"But you're the editor!" was all I could think of to say. "Don't you *want* a good article?"

Actually there was lots of other stuff I wanted to say, like, "What do you mean I don't understand him? He's a boy – of COURSE I don't understand him!" and "Why are you being so shouty?" but I was sort of too confused to say it.

"Um, I do, of course," she muttered. "It's just...it's not that easy... Oh look, Miss Kinsey's crashed the computer again. I'd better go and help her!"

And she rushed off.

After that, I worked with Alicia. And if I'm totally honest I was maybe more friendly to her, thinking that maybe Keisha would look over and think, *There is my best friend being all friendly with someone else and maybe I should not have shouted at her, oh woe, I had better say sorry.*

Only that didn't happen.

What *did* happen was this. I was working on the Rafiq article with Alicia when all of a sudden she said, "Bath, just give me your hand for a moment."

I gave her my hand, wondering what she was going to do, and do you know what, dear Diary? She got out her pen and she drew the cutest little angel on my hand!!! (Note to Miss Kinsey: that needed more than one exclamation mark! I am one of only a few people in the history of the school to be so honored!)

Wow!!

I was so moved. I felt as if I'd been initiated into a Very Special Club.

Unfortunately my delight lasted about three seconds, because there was this furious growling noise above my head, and I looked up to see Keisha standing there.

"Keisha!" I said. "Um – hello!"

But she just made a contemptuous noise and marched off!

Miss Kinsey said, "Girls, girls, control yourselves!" as Keisha slammed out of the door.

"Keish? Keisha?" I ran after her. I caught up to her in the hall. "What's the matter?"

"That Alicia and her stupid Angels! Oh, Bath, please tell me you're not going to be her friend! After I warned you not to and everything!"

I folded my arms. Keisha is my best friend, but I do NOT like the way that she always seems to think she knows what is best, dear Diary. I can make my own decisions about who to be friends with!

"Well, maybe if you explained what you've got against her, I might listen to you!"

"Can't you just trust me? Friends are supposed to trust each other!"

"Friends are *supposed* to not have secrets from each other!" I said.

Keisha blushed really hard.

"Yeah, well, I'm sorry," she said. "But it's really difficult, Bath. You don't understand. Oh – I wish I could explain! But I can't!"

And then she stomped off!

I don't want to have an argument with Keisha! She is my best friend!

Oh, I thought everything would be perfect when I had a best friend. I thought we would just keep on being friends and doing each other's hair and trading stickers and laughing about things and watching *Dramarama Diaries* together and then one day one of us would get a boyfriend and we would talk about all that too, and then we would grow up and be Movie Stars together and hang out drinking frothy milkshakes on Sunset Boulevard forever and ever!

I feel like the *Titanic* just after it hit the iceberg.

I keep wondering if I should wash the angel

off. But I don't want to! It's a really big honor – everyone keeps saying so!

And Bill is very stressed because none of the jobs he applied for gave him an interview. He is rewriting his résumé again. Bev is helping him. I heard him ask her in a sort of bitter jokey way, "How would you put a positive spin on a six-year jail sentence, then?"

So I can't tell him about me and Keisha. It would just make him more worried.

Later. Unhappy thoughts piling up in my head. Like gray clouds. Keep feeling as if I am going to rain — I mean, cry.

I keep thinking, it's HER fault for having a secret. She ought to tell me! But then I think – what if it was my secret she was keeping?

I'd want her NOT to tell anyone!

Oh, I am so miserable about it.

Evening.

Nathan is rapping outside the window! He has a CD player with all kinds of flashing lights on it, and he is bouncing up and down like the world's only ghost-pickled-onion-rapper, and he has his big sunglasses on again even though it is almost dark outside.

It is very hard to hear what he is saying because he is mumbling, and the music on the CD player is very crackly and loud.

I shouted out of the window, "I am *so* not in the mood for this, Nathan Hunderchunk!"

Bedtime.

I am lying here on my bed in my pajamas, feeling utterly miserable and hopeless, listening to the older boys outside in the distance making their car tires squeal. In the morning when you go down to the parking lot there are all these black marks on the ground where they have been doing dangerous things with their cars.

Oh, I wish Mother would call.

Later than bedtime. I am sleepless with sadness.

I was feeling so sad just now that I went downstairs to find Bill. He was making my sandwiches for tomorrow and listening to the late news. When he saw me standing there, he put down the knife and the tomato and said, "Bath, pet, what's up?"

"I neeeeeed a hug," I said, and the *need* sort of wobbled and quavered a lot.

I wondered if Bill would maybe tell me not to be silly and to go upstairs and get some sleep, but he didn't. He held out his arms and I ran into them and he gave me a ฿IG hug.

And that is the only good thing that happened today.

o   o   o   o   o   o   o   O   O

Today was HORRIBLE, dear Diary.

I sit next to Keisha in everything, and it's horrible sitting next to someone you aren't really speaking to and who you're not sure is really speaking to you but you wish they would only they don't and they borrow someone else's pencil instead of yours when they would always have usually borrowed yours because you sit next to each other because you are best friends.

Or used to be best friends.

It was like sitting next to an electric fence, when you are never sure if it is going to zap you if you touch it or not. I couldn't concentrate on any of my classes at all. All I could think about was how awful it was not

being friends with Keisha anymore. I sat
drawing sad doodles in my notebook,
and when Miss Notman asked me what four
times four hundred was, I said "Keisha" and
everyone laughed, except Keisha. (Although
for all I know that might be the right answer;
numbers stop making sense to me after about
one hundred.)

And everyone else noticed we weren't
friends too, which was even more horrible.

Like, Alicia said to me at break, "Has
Keisha stopped being friends with you? That's
so like her – never mind, you've got me!" And
she gave me a hug.

And all I could think was, *I wish Keisha
would give me a hug instead!*

And the auditions are tomorrow – I should
be practicing but I just feel too miserable.

What does it matter if I get to play Eliza,
if Keisha isn't friends with me?

What does ANYTHING matter, if Keisha

isn't friends with me?

Oh woe, woe, woe, Diary, woe.

Wednesday evening: Day of Whoopee and Wow, gods of unexpected visitors!

Natasha was just here!!!

I can't believe it! I was so happy to see her!

She came to stay with me while Bill went to the movies this evening.

I was so pleased to see her that I threw my arms around her waist and danced a tango left, right and forward over the sofa. She didn't mind at all (probably because she is not our housekeeper so she doesn't have to clean up) – she just laughed and said, "It's great to see you, Bath! I've missed you!"

This rock star she is working for is apparently incredibly famous. I had never heard of him, but Bill said, "Oh wow, yes!" and started doing air guitar like a loony, and singing, "Danannaa wwwwaaaaaawww dush dush dush," and stuff. I put my hands over my ears.

The rock star's three children are named Han, Trillian and Skywalker. He must be really quacko.

Natasha said, "How's the job-hunting going, Bill?"

Bill suddenly lost the will to air guitar.

"Not so good, to be honest," he muttered.

Natasha looked worried.

"It is important to Think Positive," I told them. "I am sure Bill will get a great job really soon now!"

After Bill had gone I practiced some lines from *Pygmalion* with Natasha. She was Professor Higgins and I was Eliza. But it made me feel sad because I kept thinking how I wasn't practicing them with Keisha. And maybe never will again, dear Diary!

I said, "Natasha, friends aren't supposed to have secrets from each other, are they?"

She said, "They're not supposed to, but sometimes they do." Then she looked at me hard and said, "I've just been over at Bev's this afternoon. Keisha was down in the dumps too. Have you two argued or something?"

"Sort of," I said sadly.

"Well, don't worry, love. These things happen, you can't expect life to be all roses. I'm sure you'll make it up eventually."

I might have talked to her more about it, but then Mother called. When she heard Natasha was there she got really prickly. "Well, where is your father? Out? I don't call that very responsible!"

She wanted Natasha on the phone, so I passed it over and then listened behind the door. I heard Natasha telling Mother what I had eaten for dinner and how many hours of TV I had watched today, and then she said very calmly, "Mrs. de Trop, I don't work for you anymore, you know."

I don't know what it was in her tone of voice, but, dear Diary, I suddenly thought, *Mother and Natasha don't like each other*.

It is completely weird that I could have gone six years living in the same house as both of them and not noticed that, and then as soon as Mother goes to America and Natasha goes to Richmond, it suddenly becomes really obvious.

I suppose Mother is pretty bossy. And I also suppose it must be strange having someone else run your whole house for you.

Interesting, dear Diary. I might even change my mind about the auditions tomorrow, and try out for the part of Mrs. Pearce, the housekeeper. I am not going to get Eliza, after all, because Alicia's cockney accent is just too good. And I know some of Mrs. Pearce's lines too.

And then the Ax Man turned up, looking for Bill, so we let him in and he had a cup of coffee and watched TV with us. It turns out that he knows how to do a cockney accent because his granny was from Bow in East London. He can do a really good "Garh!" (Not much good at the *Aaah-ooo-ooow*, though. I think you need a girl's voice for that.)

When Bill came home, and Natasha got her bag and coat, ready to leave, I suddenly felt as if I had a lump in my throat, wishing that it was the old days when she was almost always there. And not just because of the horrible argument either.

You know how you can feel like you're in the middle of two homes, sometimes? And you're not sure if you're homesick for the old one or just wishing the new one would hurry up and feel like home?

Well, maybe you don't.

But that was how *I* felt.

o   o   o   o   o   o   o   o   o

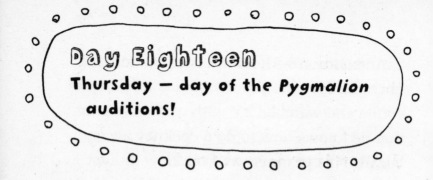

Day Eighteen
Thursday — day of the *Pygmalion* auditions!

Today Bill woke me up all early. "The job center called! I've got an interview tomorrow!" he said excitedly. "At last! Finally, someone's prepared to give me a chance!"

"Ooh, cool!" I said, jumping up and down. "What to be, what to be?"

I hoped he would say a pilot or a ski jumper or something. But no, it was Customer Services. Whatever that is. Oh well.

I was on my way to the bathroom when I remembered that the auditions are today! But I only had a second to feel excited and terrified in, before I also remembered that Keisha and me still aren't really speaking and all the excitement collapsed into misery. How

can I audition without my best friend
cheering me on???

Just after breakfast.

Oh, dear Diary!
I looked out of my window toward Keisha's
apartment, and there is a big banner
hanging out of Keisha's window.
It says, SORRY BAT.
She has clearly run out of room for the H,
but I can tell what she means.
I am going over there right now.

Break time.

I made up with Keisha. And I washed the
angel off my hand. It was so sweet of her
to hang the banner out of her window!

But she still wants me not to be friends with Alicia.

I said, "Look, Keisha, I don't think it's fair to not be friends with Alicia just because you say there's some secret thing she did that you won't even tell me. She's been really nice to me."

"Has she really, Bath? Or has she just flattered you?" Keisha looked at me hard.

I wiggled uncomfortably.

"Everyone else likes her," I retorted.

Keisha sighed. "Look, I know, Bath, that I'm not being a very good friend at the moment..."

I saw she was almost crying.

"Oh, you *are* being a good friend!" I exclaimed.

"No, I'm not, I know. I'm sorry! It's just that I'm trying to be a good friend to someone else too..."

"Oh," I said stiffly. The someone else with the secret, I suppose.

Who is this friend? Does Keisha like her more than me?

Oh, oh dear.

I don't want to be a second-best friend!

I want to be a BEST friend!

I'm going to stop thinking about this now. I have lines to remember for my audition.

Think Positive, Think Positive, Think Positive!

Later. Still no thunder. Thor possibly sick?

Keisha's audition went really well. She is so good at acting! She really, really made me believe she was old enough to be Mrs. Higgins! She is so dignified.

I bet you are wondering how my audition went too. Well, it didn't go at all, because more people auditioned for parts than we expected, and so not everyone had time to audition today in the end. Me and Alicia are going to audition tomorrow at lunchtime. I had decided to go for Eliza, but I'm having second thoughts again now that it's just me and Alicia, who is so good at her cockney accent. It would be so embarrassing if everyone laughs at my accent again. Maybe I should try out for the housekeeper after all...

The thing is, I can't imagine being the housekeeper. I can imagine being Eliza, though. I honestly think I know how she would feel, all cold and wet, selling flowers... and making jokes and being loud to pretend that she doesn't care about being out in the cold and the rain...and wishing her dad cared...and then Professor Higgins being so rude to her...and then being so nervous about acting like a princess at the ball...

But I will never get Eliza. Alicia knows all the lines by heart already.

After dinner. Still can't decide who to audition for!

Maybe I had better do some housework, so I can know what it feels like to be a housekeeper, in time for the auditions tomorrow.

I know, I will do the laundry! This will be really cool! I have never done the laundry before. And it will help Bill – he needs clean shirts for the interview tomorrow.

Half an hour later.

Wow, guess what – if you put a red sock in with white things, like shirts, everything turns pink! It is like a raspberry ripple machine out of Willy Wonka's chocolate factory.

I think I will turn *all* of our white things pink, just to see how they look. And then wash them all clean again. Tra la la...

Later. * ♡

NO ONE TOLD ME THE PROCESS WAS
IRREVERSIBLE!!!

o o o o o o o o o o

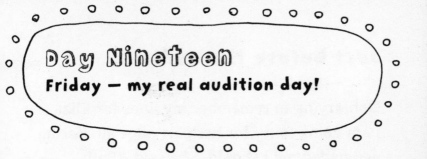

Day Nineteen
Friday — my real audition day!

Oh, dear Diary,
What a day of mixed feelings and it's not
even breakfast yet! I woke up feeling excited
because it was finally my audition. Then I saw
Bill rushing around getting ready and I
remembered his interview, so I was excited
about that too – and then I saw his PINK shirt,
and I felt SO GUILTY!

Bev says pink shirts are very trendy
nowadays and will make Bill look Sharp and
Go-Getting. I hope she is right! Oh WHY did
I think of doing the laundry?

Just before the audition.

Ooh, trying to remember my lines for Eliza...
I am going to try for her part after all. Keisha
persuaded me I should. She said, "Bath,
you're much better than you think you are!
The accent isn't the most important thing
at all."

And anyway, I don't think I am cut out
for being a housekeeper, not with the pink
shirts thing.

Nathan Hunderchunk keeps creeping
around me with the school video camera.
I know he is just doing his job, trying to make
videos of us all for the Dramarama camp
applications, but he is making me nervous!
I keep wondering if he is going to break into
a rap again.

Garn!

After the audition.

I don't think I did very well.

I tried hard, though. I just thought of how awful it was for Eliza to have everyone laughing at her accent and not knowing why. And telling her she smelled and needed a bath (I know, how mean!) I thought of how it would feel to be totally new and out of place, and having to learn a hard new accent, and trying to Think Positive despite it all. But I kept remembering the look on Bill's face when he realized his shirts had all turned pink and there was nothing he could do about it...

Alicia was SCINTILLATING (thesaurus: sparkly and brilliant) in the audition. She flounced and bounced around the stage and did a great cockney accent. I clapped with everyone else, and I am happy for her, but somehow I'm not sure if she knows how it *feels* to be Eliza. She kept looking at the audience (us) and smiling too much.

I mean, if I were Eliza, I don't think I would be so confident and bouncy. Eliza has no money for new clothes. And no money to get her clothes washed. So she smells. And if, for example, I had not got any clean school uniform because, for example, the washing machine had broken down after I had pushed two buttons at once trying to get pink clothes un-pink, I would feel just like Eliza. I would feel as if I smelled and looked horrible.

I would not feel confident and bouncy onstage, like Alicia was.

Mr. Trucillo said, "Very good, Alicia!" And then he said, "But, try and feel the character more. Forget about the audience as much as possible."

Alicia looked really shocked.

"But everyone laughed!" she said furiously.

"Well, it's not just a funny play, you know,"

he said. "It's a sad one too. Bathsheba seemed to understand that – why not get some tips from her?"

Alicia glared at him and stomped off the stage. I tried to say something nice to her as she went out, but the Angels shoved me away.

⑥

After school. Feeling a little sad because of the audition ✶ not going well...

I reread the ending of the play. I STILL think Eliza and Professor Higgins should get married! That's what's supposed to happen in romantic comedies!

I told Bill about how I wished the play had a happy ending. (He is in a very good mood because the interview went well, and – guess what – the interviewer was also wearing a

pink shirt, and on purpose! So Bev was right –
HOORAY!)

He said, "But Bath, it's a movie too, you
know. We'll rent it and watch it tonight,
okay?"

I said, "Huh, why would I want to watch
the movie when it doesn't even have a happy
ending!"

He said, "The movie is very different from
the play. It's called *My Fair Lady*. I think you'll
like it! And it'll take my mind off waiting to
hear about the job, too."

So Bill has gone out to rent *My Fair Lady,* and
ask Bev and Keisha to come over too.

Oh well, I suppose it's better than homework.

After the movie.

Dear Diary,
I LOVE *My Fair Lady*!!!

Best movie in the world, EVER!!!

There are songs! There are dances! There
are amazing, incredible, HUGE
hats! Black, white and PINK!
With feathers and ribbons
and extraordinary bows!

There are the most
wonderful costumes, like the kind of dresses
Movie Stars wear, and the Professor and Eliza
DO get together in the end! It is so much,
much, much more fun than the play.

And oh...Eliza is beautiful. Which I suppose
means I definitely won't get the part. In fact,
there is no one in the entire
school, and possibly not
even the entire world,
who is pretty enough to

be Eliza. She gets to wear a tiara, and a floaty dress, and Royalty are Amazed At Her Grace.

There are funny parts, and parts with love, and parts that make you cry. There are bouncy songs and sad songs and dancing songs. So many songs! Me and Keisha are learning the best ones by heart. We had the best time we've had in ages. We have started making hats out of cardboard!

"Maybe we can turn *Pygmalion* into *My Fair Lady*!" I said excitedly. "I could act just like Eliza in the movie, and you could act like Mrs. Higgins does, and we could make it funny, and we could maybe sing as well..."

"Oh I HOPE you get to be Eliza!" said Keisha. "You would be so good at it!"

My heart sank. I had sort of forgotten that I hadn't actually gotten the part, and probably wouldn't after all.

"Alicia will probably get it," I said.

"Oh well," said Keisha. "There's still Dramarama camp!"

Ooh, yes, dear Diary! I have been putting together a really good application. Miss Kinsey has been lots of help. I have a fantastic Supporting Statement now. It says all kinds of things about how I really feel about acting, and about how I can work as part of a team, and cope with being rejected if I fail an audition, and how I know acting is hard work, but I still want to do it...

I'm feeling excited all over again at the thought of it!

o   o   o   o   o   o   o   o   o

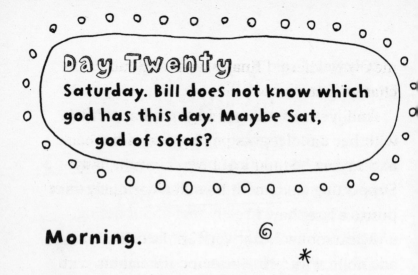

Day Twenty

Saturday. Bill does not know which god has this day. Maybe Sat, god of sofas?

Morning.

The Ax Man has fixed the washing machine! Hooray!

Afternoon.

I asked Bill for my bank card, because I wanted to buy him some new shirts, dear Diary. (I don't think he really likes pink.) The stores aren't far away. I walked there.

Nathan Hunderchunk was lurking in the men's department of the store. I think he was buying new socks. He kept popping up behind me everywhere. I finally went and hid in the changing rooms.

And just as I was coming out, I saw Alicia with her dad. He was poking her in the back and saying, "Stand up straight, young lady! How do you expect to be taken seriously with posture like that?"

Alicia looked MISERABLE. I decided not to say hello. I've felt a little uncomfortable with her ever since the auditions.

Gosh, and I thought Bev was stern sometimes!

o   o   o   o   o   o   o   O   o

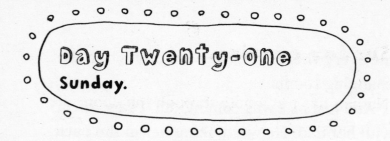

Day Twenty-one
Sunday.

Dear Diary,

I know this is going to sound really weird, but I think Nathan Hunderchunk is following me!

I've been thinking about it and all this week I have been seeing skinny black ankles disappearing around corners. And at school, every time I turn around, he is right there. Usually with his mouth open like a glupping frog.

I say, "What, Nathan? What do you want?"

And he makes a croaking sort of noise and stares at me and says, "I – I – will you –" and then runs off.

Sunday evening...

Nathan has put a note through the door!

It says:

DEAR BATHSHEBA,
I AM SORRY MY MUSIC
SHOCKED AND AWED
YOU IN THE CAFETERIA
ON TUESDAY. I JUST
WANTED TO PLAY YOU A
SPECIAL RAP I WROTE
FOR YOU.

Why would he write a rap for me, dear Diary?

How quacko!

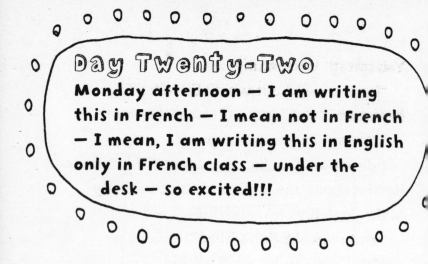

Day Twenty-Two

Monday afternoon — I am writing this in French — I mean not in French — I mean, I am writing this in English only in French class — under the desk — so excited!!!

Dear Diary,
AAAAAA!!!!!!!!!!

In fact, ah-aha-oooww-aah-ooww!!!!!!

I can't believe it!!!

I AM GOING TO BE ELIZA!!!!!

WAAA!!!!!!

I just found out this lunchtime. I was sitting in the cafeteria eating my sandwiches, when I heard Keisha screaming down the hall. She burst right into the cafeteria, knocking over Sixth Graders like bowling pins, and grabbed me by the shoulders. "You got it!!

You got it!! Waaaaaa!!"

"I got what? I got what? Expelled? A detention?"

"Noooo! The part, the part!"

I didn't know what she meant for a minute. Keisha shook me back and forth until my brain jiggled.

"You're going to be Eliza!"

"NO!"

"Yes!!!"

"What are *you* going to be?"

Dear Diary, an awful fear shot through my mind, because what if Keisha hadn't gotten a part? I thought: *Maybe I could go to Mr. Trucillo and tell him I can't be Eliza unless he gives Keisha a part too? Maybe I could start a petition in the* Clotborough Gazette *to get her a part?* But I didn't have to worry, dear Diary.

"Oh, I'm going to be a flower-seller," she said, smiling. "I actually got the part of Mrs. Higgins, but I asked if I could be a flower-seller instead, because I've got so much other stuff to do that I don't think I'll have time to learn my lines well enough."

"Oh, Keisha," I said, "that is really grown-up of you! You don't mind?"

She made a face. "Well, it was my mother's idea. It's true I *have* got lots to do, though. And I was the star last year anyway!" She gave me a big hug. "And you're the star this year!! AAAAAAA!!! WOW!!!"

We did a wild celebratory dance along the hall, met Hannah Lumb and danced hurriedly back again the other way, into a classroom, and then Miss Notman came in and said, "Y, girls, y?" So we had to stop.

But, aaaaaa! AAAAAA!!! I am going to be Eliza!!

JUBILATION, JAMBOREE, CARNIVAL AND OTHER WORDS FOR CELEBRATION!!!

I called home on Keisha's cell. Bill screamed almost as much as me, only in a deeper voice.

Bev is making us a special celebration dinner tonight, for me and Keisha and Dad and her! There is going to be gorgeous Jamaican food and English food (chips and beans). We are going to have a party!

And this isn't even the BEST thing! Mr. Trucillo called me into the computer room just before the end of lunch, and said, "Bath, you'll want to see this."

Oh, dear Diary. Nathan Hunderchunk has made the most AMAZING video of me auditioning!

There are all these special lighting effects on it. I look like a real actress! He's done close-ups and fade-ins and zooms and all kinds of things.

"I look like a Movie Star!" I whispered.

"Nathan's done a fantastic job, hasn't he?" Mr. Trucillo smiled. "He's really gotten it right with yours."

Oh, dear Diary, I want to run and find

Nathan and say THANK YOU THANK YOU THANK YOU but he isn't at school today. I am suddenly thinking of all the times he's missed school, and I never wondered where he was even though he lives opposite me. I just called him quacko.

I feel so guilty now. I feel as if I have not been a good friend to Nathan. I hope he is back at school soon, so I can say thank you to him! I wish I dared go over to his house...but I don't dare, not with Jason there.

Later — writing this in math — under desk — still excited!!

Maybe I really will get into Dramarama camp now! I don't want to be left here alone when Keisha gets in! (Because I KNOW she will – she is an acting genius!)

Uh-oh, dear Diary.

Alicia is NOT pleased about me getting the part.

She came up to me during afternoon break, and smiled at me, but it was the sort of smile that looks as if it has been shoved onto the person's mouth with a stick.

"So, great job, Bath," she said cheerfully. "Of course, I don't like to think Mr. Trucillo was biased, but you know, being a celebrity does open certain doors!"

"Oh, as if!" Keisha said. "Bath got the part because she was good!"

"You'd better watch your tongue," Alicia hissed at her. "Everyone thinks you're so perfect, but I know you're not!"

"Um...maybe we could all be friends," I said

hopefully. "Together! Three is a good number for friends!"

"Oh, you won't want to be friends with little me, now you're the star of *Pygmalion*," Alicia said, with another of those smiles.

"Yes, of course I will!"

"Oh no, you won't."

"I will!"

"You won't."

"But I wi—"

"Oh, Bathsheba, shut up!" she snapped at me. And then she Stalked off.

I have never tried Stalking before. I have never been angry enough to Stalk.

"Don't worry about her, Bath," said Keisha. "You're going to be Eliza! How amazing is that?"

I smiled back at her in a wobbly way, and then in a bigger way, because YES! I am going to be Eliza!

Can't wait for home time and the big celebration with Bill and Bev.

At home. And everything has gone wrong, wrong, wrong.

I could tell the minute I walked in with Keisha that something bad had happened. The room was sort of half-decorated for a party, but everything was quiet.

"Hello?" I said nervously.

Bev came out of the kitchen, looking really worried and upset. "Oh, girls," she said, and she gave ME a hug instead of Keisha!

"What's happened?" said Keisha, sounding really scared.

But all she said was, "Bath, go and talk with your dad, dear. He's in the living room."

Keisha gave me a quick, frightened glance. I could tell she was as worried as I was.

"What's happened?" I said in a wobbly voice. Dear Diary, suddenly all I could think of was MOTHER far on the other side of the ocean, and I rushed into the living room with my heart going *panic panic* in my chest.

Bill was sitting on the sofa looking really, really miserable.

"Oh, Bath! Congratulations!" he said, trying to smile.

"What happened?" I asked him.

"Oh, well, nothing really—"

"Dad!"

"It's all right, love. I just didn't get the job, that's all."

A rush of relief whooshed over me that it wasn't Mother being sick, and then a great rush of misery, because – Bill didn't get the job.

Dear Diary, I passed my audition. But Bill didn't pass his!

"It was the pink shirt, wasn't it?" I wailed. "It's my fault!"

"NO! Bath," he said, and so very firmly that I actually believed him. "If you must know, it was something you couldn't have done anything about – it was something that was my fault only, and nothing to do with you whatsoever!"

I feel terrible for him, dear Diary. He is trying to be cheerful, but you can see he isn't. At all.

I made him a cup of coffee. He smiled wanly and said, "You're my star, Bath. Thanks."

Then I sat next to him on the sofa and we stared at the carpet together. I tried to think of good things to say, but oh, dear Diary, what CAN one say?

It is so unfair.

He was trying so hard.

I bet it *was* the pink shirt. I am such a bad, bad daughter!

Poor, poor Bill.

Bev and Keisha went soon afterward, because there just wasn't a party atmosphere. Bev gave me a hug, and Bill a pat on the

shoulder. Keisha gave me a big hug, and then
she sort of wavered, and then she gave Bill
a hug, too. Bill looked kind of surprised, but I
think that was LOVELY of Keisha.

I went to sit on the step while Bill was inside
taking a bath to try and take his mind off it.
I saw this flitting black and white figure, and
Nathan Hunderchunk came and sat next
to me.

He glupped as if he wanted to say
something but didn't dare. I thought suddenly
that I hadn't been very nice to him. And that
made me feel even more miserable, and
guilty.

"Oh, Nathan!" I said. (Actually I think I
sobbed, rather than said.) "Thank you for
making such a good clip of me acting. Mr.
Trucillo showed it to me. It's fantastic."

He turned all pink and pleased-looking.
I think he liked being thanked, because he

actually managed to talk to me after that.
Without looking as if he thought I was going
to bite his head off.

"Are you okay?" he asked timidly.

That was kind of him, dear Diary.

"My dad didn't get a job," I said.

"Oh, my dad is always not getting jobs," he
said. "It doesn't bother him, he just goes down
the pub."

I realized that I had never seen the
Hunderchunk parents.

"Where is your dad?" I asked.

He shrugged. "My brother is home with me
most of the time. He's twenty-one, so he's an
adult. My dad's not around much."

I didn't know what to say, dear Diary. Poor
Nathan! I felt as if I wanted to tell him about
Mother hardly ever being there, and not
having a dad for years, but...I don't know.
The words were just too big to get out.

"Thank you so much for the video," I said

instead, trying to sound thankful and not miserable. "It's wonderful."

He turned very pink.

"Would you..." he began. "Would you like to – if you're not busy – I suppose you are busy – because you're spectacular – I mean—"

"What on earth are you going on about, Nathan?"

"Oh, I only wondered if one day you might like to go—"

But then the phone started ringing inside, and Bill yelled down the stairs, "Bath, could you get that, please?"

It was Mother, and by the time I got back outside, Nathan had gone.

o   o   o   o   o   o   o   o   o

Day Twenty-Three

Tuesday. We had school newspaper club today...but I didn't have any fun. I was too busy worrying.

Dear Diary,

I'm so worried about Bill. He is just sitting and sitting with his head in his hands. He hasn't been to the job center today. Nothing seems to cheer him up.

And two more bills came today. I didn't know we had to pay for water.

I don't understand why no one will give him a job!

He is brilliant!

Oh, oh, if only I had not tried the washing machine...

After school.

I meant to practice my lines for Eliza, but I just couldn't do it – I was too worried about Bill.

I just seem to make things worse. I am sure that the pinkness of his shirt can't have helped at the interview, even though he keeps telling me that is nonsense.

After dinner.

Bev came over this evening, and I heard Bill and her talking in the kitchen. When I went in they stopped quickly, but before I did I heard Bill say, "Maybe I should get another degree, maybe that would help," and Bev saying, "But Bill, where will you get the money?"

I said to Bill, "Maybe Mother would give you some money."

He said, "No."

That's all, but it was a very final "No."

I said, "You could have mine from the bank account Mother left me."

"No, Bath," he said in a different, gentler voice, "but thank you very much for offering."

It was still a very final "No," though.

o   o   o   o   o   o   o   o   o

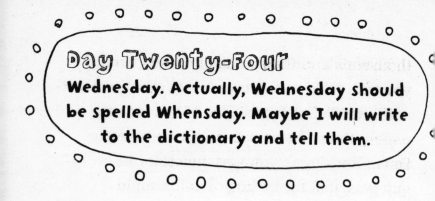

Day Twenty-Four

Wednesday. Actually, Wednesday should be spelled Whensday. Maybe I will write to the dictionary and tell them.

After dinner.

Oh no, Diary. I was watching this movie on TV called *One Last Job*. It is all about this bank robber who wants to go straight, but he needs money so he can go to college and get a job. And then one of his old Accomplices offers him thousands and thousands of dollars if he will just come and do One Last Job – which means robbing Fort Knox.

Bill wasn't watching the movie, he was reading the paper in the kitchen, so I went over and asked, "Bill, if someone offered you thousands and thousands of dollars, would you take it?"

"Take it? Good grief, yes." He shook the paper at me – there was an article about David Beckham. "Look at the cash this guy gets, just for kicking a ball around. The world's gone crazy."

"Even if they wanted you to do One Last Job?"

"Any old job would be nice right now. Why? Know someone who wants to give me one?"

"No," I squeaked, and fled upstairs, over the piano, plink-plonk, plink-plonk.

o   o   o   o   o   o   o   o   o

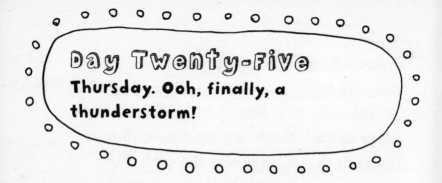

Today me and Keisha turned up to drama club
in hats we made ourselves! And we sang songs
from *My Fair Lady*, very quietly, while we
were doing our warm-up exercises onstage.

After a while, Mr. Trucillo started laughing,
and he said, "Okay, girls. I see your point. But
making the sort of scenery and costumes they
have in the movie would be a hard job,
you know."

"What are you all talking about?" said
Alicia grumpily. "And why do they keep
singing like that? It sounds stupid!"

But we didn't care what she said, because
Mr. Trucillo said that if we wanted to, we
could all watch *My Fair Lady* and see if we

wanted to act *Pygmalion* like that, instead. He went and borrowed the movie from the school library – it turns out it is a very famous movie! – and we all watched it.

It only took about five minutes before even the boys were laughing at the jokes, and Mr. Trucillo said, "Oh all right!" but in a nice way.

So we can have hats, and floaty dresses, if we are prepared to make them ourselves in our spare time, and we might possibly even get to sing songs, if Mr. Trucillo can get the music teacher to play the piano for us! Hooray for *Pygmalion*!

The only annoying thing is that Keisha STILL won't show me her cheerleading moves or let me come and watch her practice on Saturday mornings. I'm not even sure if she's tried out for the squad yet. It's really annoying, dear Diary. I don't know why she is being so quacko about it! She shows me all her macramé and she taught me to play chess, and I even went to watch her fencing once (which was very cool!).

She shares everything else, so WHY not cheerleading?

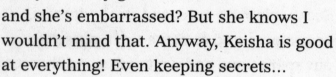

Maybe she really, really isn't any good and she's embarrassed? But she knows I wouldn't mind that. Anyway, Keisha is good at everything! Even keeping secrets...

o   o   o   o   o   o   o   o   o

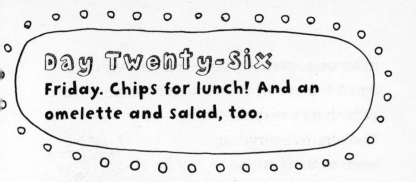

Day Twenty-Six
Friday. Chips for lunch! And an omelette and salad, too.

Dear Diary,

I am working so hard on my Dramarama application! The deadline is really soon. I have made a portfolio on the computer of all the photos and video clips that Nathan took of me, and I have written essays on *Motivation*, and *Understanding Character*, and *Overcoming Stage Fright*. Miss Kinsey helped me with all of those, and she says they are so good they could even go into the *Gazette*!

The only crummy thing is that Alicia's purse got stolen today, and she is blaming Nathan Hunderchunk.

She was making a really big fuss in the

classroom, and everyone was crowding around to see what the matter was.

"It's my new purse," she was sobbing. "It's gone, and there was my whole allowance in there!"

"Oh no, Alicia!" I said, feeling really sorry for her.

I tried to give her a hug, because after all, we are friends – at least, I *think* we are – although to be honest I haven't really known what to think since the auditions. Anyway, she shrugged me off.

"You know who did it, don't you?" she said. "That Nathan Hunderchunk! I told you, ALL the Hunderchunks are crazy! It's just the kind of thing he would do!"

"No it's not!" I said, really shocked. "I don't think he would do that at all!"

Alicia gave me this really hard look.

Dear Diary, you know when you know you

really ought to shut up, but you just CAN'T?
Well, that's what I felt like then.

"Nathan wouldn't steal anything," I said.
"Honestly, Alicia. I'm really sorry about your
purse, but it wasn't Nathan! I'm sure."

"Oh," said Alicia, very coldly. "Well, I'm
sure you'd know all about it."

"I am really sorry about your purse, Alicia,"
I said miserably.

She suddenly gave me a lovely smile. I
mean, I think it was meant to be lovely. But it
felt a little fake.

"I know. Never mind. I'm sure the criminal
will get caught. Don't they always?"

After school. ⑥

I thought Alicia was going to be all normal and
nice after she smiled at me...but now
I'm not so sure. Because during afternoon

break, she said to me, "Is it true your dad went to prison?"

I muttered something, and she said, "Oh, you *poor* thing. It must be *soooo* difficult for you. Never knowing when he might commit a crime again."

"He wouldn't ever do it again!"

She sort of raised her eyebrows and then she gave me a big hug, and said, "Of course he won't! Definitely not! Because, like I said, criminals always get caught. I bet he would never put you through all that stress, you know, of seeing him dragged out of the house and into a police car, and—"

I said, "Alicia, shut up."

Her sharp eyes sort of flashed. But she didn't say anything else.

o   o   o   o   o   o   o   o   o

Day Twenty-Seven
Saturday. Dear Diary, horrible developments!!!

Dear Diary,

I have had a horrible experience! It has probably scarred me for life!!

Just after lunch, there was a knock at the door, and Bill answered it. I didn't hear anyone saying anything, but the next thing I knew, Bill called up the stairs, "Someone to see you!" and someone was knocking on my door.

I thought, *Ooh, Keisha!* so I shouted, "Come in!"

Not Keisha, dear Diary. It was Nathan Hunderchunk, of the looming socks and the flashing kitchen timers!

I just happened to be rehearsing Eliza,

☆ 215 ☆

and I had the curtains tucked into my underwear (a long story, dear Diary; let me just say it is hard to improvise an evening dress, okay?) and I really, REALLY was not expecting to see Nathan Hunderchunk. I sort of shrieked, and entangled myself further in the curtains by mistake. Nathan stood by the door looking terrified.

"Are you...are you...okay...?" he managed to say.

I managed to get myself out of the curtains, and collapsed on the bed.

"Yes! I mean – yes! Of course!"

"You have a piano stuck in your hall."

"What? Oh! Yes – I know!"

Great, dear Diary. Now I have made Nathan Hunderchunk, the quacko-est boy in the school, think I am even quacko-er than him.

"What do you want, Nathan?" I said, trying to get back some dignity, as I stood up on the bed. "I am awfully busy, rehearsing."

"I just...I wanted to say thank you for sticking up for me, to Alicia. For saying I didn't steal her purse. Rafiq told me how nice you were about it."

"Oh!" I smiled at him in a Princesscular fashion, very Gracious and Kind. "You're welcome. I know you wouldn't do that."

He was still standing there, sort of shifting from one foot to another.

"I wondered if...I wondered if..."

"What, Nathan?" I said, trying not to be impatient.

"Well...just if one day...you might like to go on a date."

Dear Diary, I was Struck Dumb. And Dumb Struck.

"I have two tickets to the Computer Programming Championships," he said eagerly. "It's really interesting and mathematical!"

I gaped at him, in Pure Horror.

"I thought maybe—"

"No!" I shrieked. "Nathan Hunderchunk, ABSOLUTELY NOT!"

Dear Diary, when I told Bill, he said that was a really HORRIBLE thing to say. And he is right. But my mouth was just out of my control!

Poor, poor Nathan! He just ran out of the bedroom, and I stood there on the bed feeling worse and worse and WORSE.

AUGH!

I feel terrible!

You see, Diary – it's hard to explain, but you're my diary so I know you'll understand – the thing is, I always thought that one day, in a future far, far away, when I am finally a Glamorous Movie Star and am maybe about sixteen, I *would* have a boyfriend to go on dates with. But – don't laugh, dear Diary – I always thought he would be someone like Brad. You know, Bathsheba-in-the-books' boyfriend. Tall and handsome and not with a head like a pickled onion. And he would definitely not want to go to Computer Programming Championships, but to Glittering Movie Premieres instead.

I just never IMAGINED Nathan would ask me on a date.

I mean, to go from Brad (even though he doesn't exist) to Nathan Hunderchunk is kind of a shock.

Also, what about all those circuit board thingies he keeps giving me?! That is quite a quacko act. If I ever have a boyfriend I think he ought to give me chocolate. (Or maybe flowers, but preferably chocolate.) Not circuit boards, anyway, especially used ones.

Oh dear, oh dear, but I was still very rude to Nathan.

"You ought to go over and apologize," said Bill. He was very stern, dear Diary! "Honestly, girls have no idea how much they hurt boys' feelings sometimes!"

"But I never want to see him again!"

I really did feel, just then, as if I never did want to see him again, dear Diary. Although of course I do. I just don't want to go on a date with him! Especially not to something mathematical!

"That has nothing to do with it! Bathsheba, you were really rude."

So I have written him a note. It says:

Dear Nathan,
I am sorry I said absolutely not. What I meant to say is that I'm afraid I really do not ever want to go out with you, ever, but thank you very much for asking, but please do not ever ask again, ever.
  I am very sorry I hurt your feelings.
Sorry.
Bathsheba Clarice de Trop

I am going to put it in his locker at school.
I do not dare put it in his mailbox – I think the
horrible dogs would eat it. Or Jason would.

o o o o o o o o o

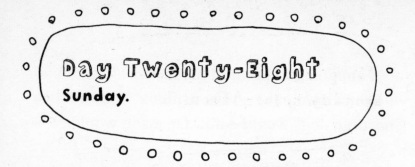

Today Bill took me and Keisha to the stables, to ride Poppy and Pepper, my two ponies. It was so nice to see them again! I haven't seen them for ages.

I rode Poppy (the black one with the white star) and Keisha had her first try at riding ever, on Pepper (the chestnut one). She hung on really tight, but she was smiling so much, I think she really enjoyed it. I showed her how to put the tack on, and take it off, and how to rub Pepper down afterward.

I told her about Nathan Hunderchunk, too.

"Ponies are much nicer than boys!" I said. "Who would want a boyfriend anyway? Yuck!"

Keisha turned red, but I am sure she agrees.

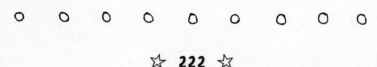

Day Twenty-Nine
Monday. Before school.

Really anxious about today, dear Diary.
I hope Nathan Hunderchunk doesn't do
anything quacko.

Lunchtime.

Well, Nathan has not looked at me once all
day, which I am kind of glad about (but also
kind of not). He just scurries off when he sees
me coming. So I put the note in his locker
(sort of squidged in down the gap between the
door and the wall). I hope he finds it! And I
hope it makes him feel better. Poor Nathan!
I do like him – only not in THAT way.

Afternoon break. ＊ ⑥

I started worrying that my note was not nice
and apologetic enough. I would hate for
Nathan to think I was horrible! So I wrote
another one, and stuck that in his locker, too.

The new note said:

> Dear Nathan,
> I really am sorry that I do not
> want to go out with you in the
> slightest, ever. But I think you
> make very nice videos and
> kitchen timers and things, and
> you have great talent as a rapper
> and will go far.

(The last part is not true, dear Diary, but I
got sort of carried away by wanting to be nice
to him.)

After school.

Found a note in MY locker!
It said:

WOULD IT MAKE
A DIFFERENCE IF
I WAS GOOD-
LOOKING AND
SPORTY LIKE
RAFIQ?

I wrote him a note back.
It said:

No.

o o o o o o o o o

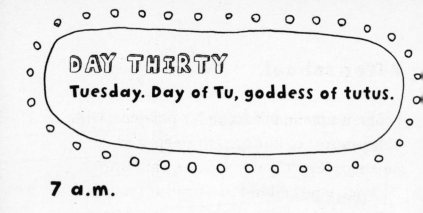

DAY THIRTY
Tuesday. Day of Tu, goddess of tutus.

7 a.m.

Oh, no, dear Diary. Nathan is rapping outside the house again.

I pushed my head under the pillow, but I can still hear him...

"Bathsheba! You're a superstar!
You're more than great, you're
spec-tac-u-lar!
You are the best; you beat the rest –
I have written your name on my
second-best vest!"

He has, too, dear Diary. In black marker. I can see it when I peek through the curtains.

7:05 a.m.

...Bill has just come in, in his pajamas, with his eyes sort of blurry with sleep, and moaned, "Can't you make him shut up?"

"Well, you said not to be rude to him!"

Bill said something very angry, and went back out of the room. I think he banged his knee on something on the landing, too. He yelled out of the window, "Bathsheba is too young for a boyfriend!"

Dear Diary, this is the most embarrassing moment of my life.

7:15 a.m.

Mr. Kapoor has thrown a samosa at Nathan!

7:16 a.m.

Nathan is eating the samosa!

7:30 a.m.

Nathan has finally gone, leaving just samosa crumbs behind him.

And now I have to get up, and go to school, where I hope I do not see him!

After school, very tired, because I did not get enough sleep this morning.

Well, dear Diary, we have put the first issue of the *Clotborough School Gazette* to bed!

That is what it is called when everything is wrapped up and finished, and you print off the newspaper and it is all hot from the photocopier!

We made one hundred and fifty copies, and my "Being Bathsheba" article is on page one of all of them!!! And my Rafiq interview is on the back with the Sports Round-Up.

Wow.

I feel so happy and proud. I am going to mail a copy to Mother in America, so she can see how famous I am already!

I can't believe I've been a school girl for a whole month! It has been really exciting, but not in the way I expected it to be at all. I thought there would be at least one Hockey Cup stolen by now. Oh well – there's plenty of time!

Miss Kinsey bought us cookies to celebrate, so it was late by the time we had finished. Keisha was really tired – even Miss Kinsey said she had worked really hard on the issue, and deserved a gold star. But we didn't have a gold star, so we went home and watched *Dramarama Diaries* instead.

"That could be us, next summer," said Keisha, as we watched it. It could, dear Diary! I am really proud of my Dramarama camp application. I *might* get in, I really think I might! And if I do, I might be one of the ones they pick to film! And then I would REALLY be a star!

○   ○   ○   ○   ○   ○   ○   ○   ○

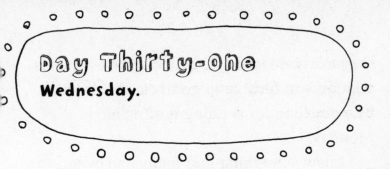

Day Thirty-one
Wednesday.

Dear Diary,
DISASTER!!!

The school computers have been stolen!!!

Sorry, Miss Kinsey, but right now I need all the exclamation marks I can get, as well as the thesaurus.

It is a CATASTROPHE DISASTER CALAMITY UPHEAVAL DEVASTATION CATACLYSM, which are all words that sound like pots and pans clattering and clashing and falling and smashing and basically being in the middle of an earthquake that destroys everything you ever dreamed of!!!!!

Because all our Dramarama camp applications were on the computer and they are gone, gone, GONE!!! There is no way we will be able to go to camp this year. The deadline for sending it off is next Monday!

I knew something had happened even before I got to the classroom. I could hear Alicia shouting, and the sound of crying, and I just somehow knew it was Keisha crying. I RAN down the hall, and burst into the classroom – and there was Keisha, in tears, and Alicia shouting, and everyone else just huddled around miserably.

"What's happened? Keisha?"

"It's not my fault!" Keisha sobbed.

"Yeah, but," Alicia said furiously, "you know it was you who locked the door to the computer room last night. Or DID you lock it? Maybe you just didn't lock it right, and that's how they got in, and—"

"What are you talking about?" I shouted.

And that's when Keisha told me the

computers were gone. And everyone was blaming her.

I bet you are thinking, *How could it be Keisha's fault?* and the thing is this: Miss Kinsey forgot to lock the door to the computer room after newspaper club, and we were halfway down the hall when she remembered. So…she said to Keisha, "Run back and lock it for me, would you, dear?" And she gave her the keys. And Keisha ran back and locked the door.

And now people are saying that it is Keisha's fault because she didn't lock the door right.

"That's nonsense!" I shouted back at Alicia. "Miss Kinsey asked Keisha to lock the door because she's the most responsible, and you know that! There's no way she wouldn't have locked the door right. And anyway, the thieves broke into the school! How is that Keisha's fault?"

That shut people up. And then Miss Kinsey

came in, and she'd obviously heard what we were saying, because she said, VERY sternly, "I don't want anymore of this blaming Keisha nonsense. If anything, it's my fault!"

"It's not your fault, Miss Kinsey," I said, but very miserably.

Because it doesn't matter whose fault it is.

The Dramarama applications are gone.

o   o   o   o   o   o   o   o   o

Day Thirty-Two
Thursday.

Dear Diary,

Things are just getting worse and worse!

When I came into school this morning, there was a big group of people around Alicia and Chanelle and Davina. And they all turned around when I came in. And they were all smiling.

"Bath! We're so glad you're here!" called out Alicia.

I looked at her suspiciously.

She waved a copy of a newspaper at me. Our newspaper. The *Clotborough School Gazette*.

"I'm so glad that you're going to save the day," she said, smirking. "By finding the computers."

"Oh?" I said.

"Yes, you are – just as you promised." She handed me the paper.

Dear Diary, I read these words. MY words.

I expect that something awful will happen like someone stealing the Hockey Cup because that always happens in books about school — anyway, it does in the books my mother writes. In that case, have no fear!!! I will catch the thief!!!

Dear Diary, why do I not just learn to keep my mouth SHUT???

"You'd better get started then, Bath," said Chanelle, grinning at me.

"Right..." I said weakly.

Catch a thief, dear Diary?

How on EARTH am I going to go about doing that?

"Yeah, we told everyone that you'd been

showing off that you could solve any crime," said Davina.

"Thanks…" I muttered.

"Good luck with your investigation, Nancy Drew," said Alicia. And she gave me a poisonous sort of snaky smile.

I sat down at my desk and did not pay attention at all for the rest of the day, dear Diary. I was far, far too busy worrying. And feeling awful, because it is clear to me now that Alicia is NOT my friend at all. Not after she was so horrible to Keisha yesterday, and today, so horrible to me.

It did not help that people kept coming up to me and saying, "Nice one, Bath. Well done, it's so cool of you to catch the thief for us!"

After school, and after drama club.

I am trying to think who could have done it.
There is a big rumor going around that it was
an international gang of mastermind criminals
who stole the computers. But all day there have
been millions of rumors, including one that Mr.
Baxter-Bix did it and sold the computers and
went on a Caribbean cruise, which is not true
because I saw him in his office.

And a policeman named Steve came to see
the school newspaper club people during lunch
hour. I thought I might get some hints from
him, but I didn't.

Steve looked at us all really hard, and said,
"If any of you saw anything suspicious –
anything at all – you must tell your teacher
and she will let us know. You don't have to
tell us your name. But this is a serious theft,
of equipment worth thousands. We need your

help on this." And then he went on about the School Community and the Wider Community and Moral Responsibility and stuff.

He was really nice, dear Diary. I don't know if this is a good thing to think or not, but... I was glad he didn't know my dad was once in prison.

No one had any motivation at drama club. Most people were just moaning about not getting to go to Dramarama camp, and the ones who weren't were gossiping about the computers. I refused to look at Nathan – it would only be cruel to encourage him. Yuck, yuck, yuck.

Mr. Trucillo said, "I know how disappointing this is for you. But – I would think you've all heard the phrase 'The Show Must Go On'?"

We all nodded and muttered "Yes".

"Well, now's the time to make that old saying come true! We'll still do our new and improved version of *Pygmalion*, Dramarama camp or no Dramarama camp. And it will be the best show this school has ever seen, because you guys are professionals!"

"We're just kids," objected one of the boys.

"And we're not getting any money for it," said Alicia. (She's in the play too – she plays a fancy lady named Clara.)

"Professional isn't about how old you are, or how much you earn, it's an attitude! I've seen how dedicated you have all been to learning your lines and working as a team. Going on in the face of disaster – that's being a professional too. Actors have to do that all the time! I know you are going to make me proud."

Well, that did make me feel good, dear Diary. As good as I possibly could feel, under the circumstances.

o · o o o o o o o o

Day Thirty-Three
Friday.

3 a.m.

How on earth can I catch the thief?

6 a.m.

Okay. I am really, really tired, but I had better make a list of suspects at least.

People are expecting things of me!

List of Suspects
☆ An international gang of Criminal Masterminds
☆ Mr. Baxter-Bix
☆ A bad man who happened to be passing by
☆ A bad woman who happened to be passing by
☆ The Computer Liberation League

Yes, dear Diary. Even I know those are stupid ideas!

Lunchtime.

Keisha said, "You don't have to do it, Bath! Everyone knows you're not really a detective."

I said, "No, they don't! They think I'm just like Bathsheba in the books – at least the Eighth Graders do. Anyway, Alicia just wants me to fail! I can't give up. I've got to at least try."

"But why, Bath?"

I thought hard. Then I said, "It's like doing an audition that you're worried you're going to fail at. It's braver to give it a try than not even try at all."

"That's true," said Keisha. "And look how you got the part of Eliza without ever expecting to!"

Yes, dear Diary.

But I have no time to practice my lines –
I have to catch this thief!

And Nathan keeps bothering me. I just
don't have time for it. I told him to go away
and then I hid in the girls' bathroom so he
couldn't find me.

Later. At home.

Hmm.

So...suspects might be anyone who has
motivation. Or anyone who has opportunity.

Well, I don't know who would have
opportunity. Anyone who was around the
school in the middle of the night, I suppose.

How on earth am I supposed to find out
who was around the school in the middle of
the night?

Okay. Move on to motivation.

Well, why would anyone steal computers? To sell them and make money, probably.

So...motivated people = someone who needs more money.

Oh, well that could be anyone.

I mean, Bill needs more money, for heaven's sake.

Oh no, dear Diary. I've just had a horrible thought.

What if he is doing One Last Job?

I feel terrible for even thinking it. I know it isn't true. Bill would never do that. No way. Not in a million years. I keep thinking, *Nonsense, Bathsheba*, and also thesaurus words for nonsense, such as POPPYCOCK and BALDERDASH. But now I've thought it, I can't get it unthought.

I feel as if my stomach is sort of sloshing around my shoes in a cold, worried, not-wanting-it-to-be-true soup.

Cleaner...but no wiser.

I put the pen down and went for a bath.

I floated Quacko Duck on my tummy.

"Dear Quacko," I told it, "I must be a terrible daughter! How could I even think such things about Bill!"

I finished my bath and went downstairs full of sorrow and worry. Bill looked at me and frowned.

"What is the matter with you?" he asked. "You look as if you've got the world on your shoulders."

"So do you," I said reproachfully.

"Huh. I'm just worried about finding a job. To tell the truth, Bath –" he took a deep breath – "it's not going so well."

"I know," I said, "but I don't see why."

"Some people, well...don't want someone who was once a criminal working for them."

"But you said you were sorry. You've been to prison."

Bill shrugged.

"Yeah, but...sometimes it's hard for people to trust you again," he said, very sadly.

I felt bad then, because I knew I had not been trusting him either. I looked at him, and I suddenly knew, absolutely, without a shadow of a doubt, that he had not taken the computers. No way. Not Bill.

I gave him a big hug.

He laughed. "What's that for?"

"For being a great dad," I told him. "You *will* get a job. I'm sure of it. I believe in you!"

Late evening.

Someone has rung the doorbell and run away!

Three times!

The third time it happened, Bill shouted out

of the door, "Do that again and I'll call the cops!"

I think I saw a white tracksuit disappearing toward the Hunderchunk house.

o o o o o o o o o

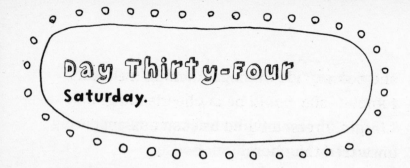

Dear Diary,

I don't think I have ever had such a week in my life.

You know how you think things can't get worse? And then they do?

And then you find out that they can get even worse than that?

And then something ELSE happens – and things suddenly turn out to be totally crazy?

I am writing this on Saturday night, because I was just FAR TOO BUSY to even think about writing any of it down at the time. But. Here we are, and I think I am FINALLY calm enough to try writing it down!

Well, this morning I called Keisha, to see if

she had any ideas about catching the thief. I know – she would be at cheerleading, but I forgot. I remembered as soon as Bev answered the phone.

"Oh, sorry – I forgot Keisha's at cheerleading," I said, and was going to say bye and put the phone down, except Bev said, "Cheerleading? What do you mean? She's gone to the library to work, Bath."

"Oh," I said, very slowly. But my brain was going very, very fast.

The library? So had she given up cheerleading? But then why hadn't she told me?

Had she just forgotten?

But Keisha usually tells me everything – except her big secret.

Bev said, "Is everything all right, love?"

"Oh!" I said again. "Yes, thanks!" and then I put the phone down.

I didn't know WHAT to think.

All I knew was that I was going to the library. And I wish I could say I truly expected to find Keisha there!

On the way to the library I was thinking all these awful things about what Keisha might be up to. I was worried about her and angry with her and scared too.

I went inside the library. No Keisha. I looked everywhere. Even in the Reference section. And that's when I heard the voices.

It was Alicia. I remembered how she had been in the library with her dad, before. But I didn't think her dad was there now, because she was whispering and giggling with someone, which I don't think her dad would let her do.

"Really," I heard her say. "Her father killed someone. That's why he went to prison."

I moved a little closer. I wondered who they were talking about so nastily. I suddenly thought, *I really, really don't like Alicia.*

"But she's so rich!" That was Chanelle. "Is her dad *really* a criminal?"

Alicia laughed. "Oh, Bathsheba's not that rich really. She lives in this horrible little house – right opposite the crazy Hunderchunks. Yeah, her dad definitely killed someone. It was all over the newspapers!"

I felt as if my head was whirling and spinning all around. I took a deep breath. I just couldn't believe what I was hearing.

I stepped out from behind a bookcase. Alicia looked up, and I saw her expression change as she saw me.

"Oh, Bath!" she said. "Hello! We were just...er..."

Chanelle and Davina were staring at me, with huge, horrified eyes. I swallowed.

"You know that's not true!" I said, and my voice came out a lot more wobbly than I'd meant it to. "It's not true, Alicia! It's a lie!"

"What?" She shrugged and looked at me innocently.

"What you said. About my dad. It's not true."

Alicia looked away as if she was bored, or embarrassed, I'm not sure which, dear Diary.

"Oh well," she said. "Who cares?"

Dear Diary, I just had no idea what to say to her. I mean, I knew she gossiped, but I thought at least she thought the stories she told were true!

I just turned around and walked off. I always seem to do that! Run off when I'm upset, I mean. Maybe I shouldn't. But I just couldn't bear to look at Alicia.

I couldn't face going back through the library with everyone looking at me, either. I felt as if I'd been hit in the chest, and I could feel tears running down my face. I saw there was a door marked *Fire Exit*, and I pushed it open and went out. There was a fire escape outside, and about halfway down, two people were sitting, side by side, looking at each other in a very soppy way.

Keisha – and Rafiq.

Dear Diary, I just stood there, holding on to the railing of the fire escape. My tears dried up completely. I think it was the shock.

They hadn't seen me at all.

I heard Keisha say, "But Raff, I hate having to keep it a secret."

So this was it, dear Diary! Keisha's big secret was – Rafiq!

And all I could think was, *He couldn't even give me a decent interview.* HUH!

I put my hands on my hips. *Right!* I thought. *No more running off for Bathsheba Clarice de Trop! I am going to Stand and Fight!*

"So THIS is the big secret!" I said stormily. "Or do you have MORE secrets, huh? BEST FRIEND??"

Keisha shrieked and turned around, and Rafiq jumped up, looking shocked. As soon as Keisha saw it was me, she hung her head and started to say something, but Rafiq butted in.

"Look, Bathsheba, it's not Keisha's fault. It's mine. She didn't want to keep it a secret, but I made her."

He sighed and shoved his hands into the pockets of his hoodie.

"Thing is," he muttered, "my parents are really strict. They'd kill me if they found out I have a girlfriend."

"Oh? Well, who says I'd tell them?" I had to grit my teeth to stop myself from shaking with anger.

Keisha looked at me pleadingly.

"Bath, we didn't think you'd tell on purpose, but sometimes you seem so friendly with Alicia," she said, "and if you let it slip to her, well, the whole school will know in about five seconds! She hates, hates, hates Raff!"

"No, they would not, because I would never tell Alicia – she is so *not* my friend! You were totally right about her, Keisha," I said, suddenly realizing she had been right from the very beginning. "I'm sorry I didn't trust you."

"No, I'm sorry I didn't trust you with the secret!"

"Yeah, you should be!"

"We didn't tell *anyone*, Bath. It's not just Raff's parents, you see. It's my mother, too. Bath, I was really scared she'd stop me from going to all my clubs if she found out I was spending time with Raff instead of studying. You know how strict she can be!"

This is true, dear Diary. Bev is really nice, but when it comes to Homework and Concentrating On Your Studies…well, she sort of turns into a monster. I suddenly realized that Keisha had probably been feeling just as upset as me over keeping the secret.

"I'm so sorry, Bath," she said miserably.

"Oh, Keisha, I forgive you!"

"Oh, Bath!"

We fell into each other's arms. Rafiq rolled his eyes. "When you ladies have finished," he said.

"Why does Alicia hate Rafiq anyway?" I asked. "Or *is* there another secret?"

Keisha glanced at Rafiq and he said, "Yeah, go ahead, she knows everything else anyway."

"Well, look, this can never go any further than you and me and Raff, okay, Bath?"

I nodded hard. One thing I do NOT do, Diary, is spread gossip! I have had enough of that from mean Alicia!

"Well, last year, Alicia asked Raff out," said Keisha.

"No!!"

"Yes! And he said no. She was *really* annoyed. And then – guess what – she only went and got Hannah Lumb to beat him up!"

Rafiq looked horribly embarrassed.

"Please," he begged me, "never ever tell anyone that. If it gets out I got beaten up by a girl..." He shuddered.

"I've got a nightmare Alicia story too!" I told them what I had just overheard in the library. As I came to the end, I looked at Keisha and I actually started to get really scared. I'd never seen her so angry. Her nostrils were actually getting white and pinched and her eyes were glittering like a lioness's or something.

"It's okay," I said hurriedly. "I mean, it doesn't matter! Honestly. I'm over it now! Keisha? Keish?"

"THAT ALICIA ABEBE!" she exploded. I actually ducked, and Rafiq flinched, and looked terrified. "That is just the WORST,

NASTIEST... Oh! Oh! Oh!" She jumped up with her fists clenched and steamed around like a balloon when you let the air out. "I'm going to teach her a lesson!"

"Don't hurt her!" I squeaked. I looked at Rafiq and he looked at me and he was obviously thinking the same thing as me, which was *Help!!!*

"I'm going to – I'm going to – oh! Come with me!" She grabbed my wrist and stormed off, and I was dragged along behind, like a suitcase or something. Rafiq ran after us. We went back into the library, but Alicia wasn't there anymore. Just Chanelle and Davina, whispering and looking really stressed.

"Where's Alicia?" demanded Keisha.

"She went home," said Chanelle.

"Yeah, she was really upset when Bathsheba was so mean to her," added Davina, giving me a poisonous look.

"Oh!" I said furiously. But I had no chance

to defend myself, because Keisha was storming off through the library, and I had to follow her because she was still attached to my wrist like a handcuff!

Eventually we got to a house I've never been to before, a little outside the neighborhood. It had a very neat lawn, with plants in neat rows as if they had been planted by someone who wasn't afraid to use a ruler.

"Keisha, what are we doing here?" Rafiq asked. But Keisha was already ringing the doorbell. It wasn't until her father answered the door that I realized this was Alicia's house.

"Yes?" he said, glaring at us as if we were really, really not welcome.

"I want to speak to Alicia, please," said Keisha.

"She's doing her homework."

"It's important," said Keisha.

Mr. Abebe gave Keisha a very hard look, and then called up the stairs in a different

language. Alicia came rushing down after
a few seconds. She looked really surprised,
a little scared, and not at all pleased to see us
there. She came out and stood on the step.

"Five minutes," her father said to her. "Then
back to algebra!"

Alicia nodded. Her father gave us a last,
lingering *I'll be back...* kind of look and then
melted into the shadows of the house like
a vampire.

"Keisha," said Alicia, uncomfortably.

Keisha glared at her. "Alicia," she responded.

It was like two lionesses prowling and
growling around each other... only not in
Africa, but in a rainy street in London.

"What do you want?" said Alicia.

"I want to tell you a few things. You may
think you're really smart and you have the
school under your thumb. But we're not going
to put up with your two-faced bullying
anymore. We've had enough! Bath knows

what you're really like now, and we aren't scared of you anymore."

"Oh yeah?" Alicia sneered. Then she looked at Rafiq. "What's he doing here?"

Rafiq looked embarrassed. "I came along in case Keisha needed defending."

Alicia snorted. "You can't even defend yourself!" Then she looked at Keisha (who did not look as if she needed defending, dear Diary). Alicia's eyes suddenly went wide. "Oh – I get it!" she said. "Hah! I *knew* there was something going on! Keisha and Rafiq, sitting in a tree, K-I-S-S-I—"

"Oh shut up!" said Keisha and Rafiq at the same moment.

Alicia made a face at us. "Well, well. What if I tell your parents about you? Bet yours would be *really* pleased to know what was going on, Rafiq."

Keisha drew herself up to her full height (she's really tall for her age, dear Diary).

"And what if I let slip to *your* parents about the lie you were spreading about Bathsheba's dad?" Keisha retorted. "I'll call your dad right now, shall I? And, oh yeah, I could also tell him how you hide gossip magazines inside your math textbook."

Alicia didn't say anything. She looked pale, though.

"Yeah, you just think about it," said Keisha. "And stay out of the way of me and my friends!"

And then she swept off. Like a lioness that had just gutted a jackal.

I glanced at Rafiq, and we both looked at Alicia. She was still standing on the step, looking kind of sick.

Then we RAN after Keisha.

So THAT, dear Diary, was my day today!

I have discovered that someone I once thought was my friend is actually my worst enemy.

I have discovered that my best friend has a secret boyfriend.

And I have seen my best friend in Lioness Action Style!

No wonder I am absolutely exhausted.

I finally presented Keisha with the Friend Medal. For services to her friends. Above And Beyond The Call Of Duty.

She blushed.

"I don't deserve this, Bath!"

"Yeah you do! You did your best to be a good friend, not just to me but to Raff too – so you deserve it twice over."

o   o   o   o   o   o   o   O   o

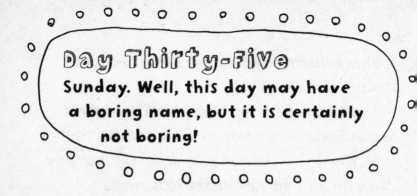

Day Thirty-Five

Sunday. Well, this day may have a boring name, but it is certainly not boring!

Dear Diary,

Why can't I have just one normal day?!!

I spent the whole day on the computer, looking up ways to catch thieves. But they all seem to need fingerprints, or security cameras. And the school computer thieves didn't even leave any cigar butts at the scene, so I can't trace them to a small village in Mexico, like in *Bathsheba and the Jaguar's Tail*. I decided to go for a walk to try and make my brain work better.

"I'm going out for a walk, Dad!" I shouted as I left the house. I walked up to the merry-go-round and went around on it a few times, in case it stirred up my thinking, but it didn't. I still had NO idea how to catch the thief.

I came back home feeling really worried. Well, dear Diary, it was nothing compared to how worried I was going to be in another five seconds! Because I unlocked the door and walked into the house and walked into the kitchen to find Bev there. And Bill was – wait for it – KISSING HER.

To be exact, Bill had just punched the air, yelled, "Hooray!" and then flung his arms around Bev and kissed her on the mouth. And Bev looked confused and startled but pleased. And then she saw me. Staring at them.

I don't know why, but I just burst into tears. "Bathsheba!"

I felt awful when I saw Bev's face, because she looked so guilty. I mean, if I could choose anyone in the world for Bill to get together with, I wouldn't mind Bev at all. But I just wasn't expecting it. I tried to explain all this but my face was too busy crying.

"Bath!" Bill rushed to me. Bev hovered in the background looking horrified.

Dear Diary, all I could think of to say (or rather sob) was "I'm a gooo-oo-d girl, I am!"

Honestly, sometimes I think I am slightly quacko.

"I'm so sorry, so sorry," Bev said. "I should go. I'm so sorry, Bath."

Bill gave me a huge hug, and then I just heard the door closing behind Bev.

"I wouldn't mind having Keisha for a sister," I sobbed. "But promise you won't like her more than me?"

(I actually don't know if I meant Bev or Keisha, by "her," it was all kind of confused.)

"Bath! What an idea!" Bill looked horrified. "Of course I wouldn't love anyone more than you – anyway, it's a totally different thing."

"I don't think I am a good daughter," I sobbed. "I've never done any housework before. I didn't mean to conflagrate your shirts!"

"Oh, Bath! I'd love you even if you burned down the house – but don't try it," he added hurriedly.

I laughed. Which might have been his intention. Parents can be sly like that.

"Why didn't you tell me about you and Bev?"

"To tell you the truth – it's never happened before. It wasn't meant to happen then! Bev is a great friend, but..." He trailed off. "Bath, adult lives are sometimes very complicated," he said. "But the main thing is, me and Bev both love you and wouldn't want to upset you at all, ever."

(Huh!! If he thinks ADULT lives are complicated, he should try being practically a teenager!!)

"The fact is – I got a little carried away there because, well, because I've got a job!" He grinned at me.

"No! Really?"

"Yes! I'm going to work for Bev's cousin in his computer repair business! Good wages, good hours – it's perfect!"

"That's wonderful!" I said. "Amazing!"

But I just couldn't summon up the energy to do a little dance or anything. I was feeling too overwhelmed.

"What's the matter?" Bill asked. "You look worn out, Bath. You've been looking stressed for ages. Come on – no secrets from your dad."

Dear Diary, I wish it was that easy! I thought about what I could and couldn't tell him. I wasn't going to tell him about the Alicia stuff, because it was over now, and it would only be more stress for him (in his complicated adult life – huh!). So instead I said, "Nothing." Which sounds as if it should sound cool and elegant, but actually just sounded sad and sorry for itself.

Bill put his arm around me. "What do *you*

want, Bath? What are you missing?"

"I want to go to Dramarama camp. But that will never happen. The applications have to be in tomorrow, and I still haven't found the school computers!"

He sighed. "Bath, it's not up to you to do that. It's out of your hands, now. Anything else?"

I thought really hard.

Dear Diary, I have most things I want.

I have a dad who loves me.

I have a best friend who sticks up for me like a lioness.

I don't have Alicia for a friend and I expect she will try to be mean to me at school – but that's her problem!

(Huh, I wonder if she has a diary. Maybe it is covered in pictures of snakes and other poisonous little animals. And maybe she

writes things like "Today I made someone's life a misery. Bwa-ha-ha-ha-haaa!")

"No!" I wailed. "The only thing I really want is to find the computers, so I can go to Dramarama camp!"

Later.

Dear Diary,
Astonishing developments!

I was just drawing up a new list of suspects when there was a knock at my bedroom door. I hadn't even heard anyone coming into the house, I had been concentrating so hard, and I was not expecting to see Nathan Hunderchunk in front of me!

"Nathan!" I said nervously, and dropped my pen, and got ink all over my notes. *Oh no, I thought, does he want to ask me out again?*

"Bathsheba," he said, and I realized he

looked really, really worried, dear Diary.
"Please will you come over to my house?
I need to show you something."

I didn't know what to say, dear Diary.
Jason–dogs–eek went through my mind.
But Nathan looked really, really unhappy.

"Please – I need your help!" he said.

Dear Diary, you will never guess what he
wanted help about.

We went over to Nathan's house. He
insisted on creeping through the bushes as if
we were spies or something, even though he
said Jason and the dogs were definitely out.

"I've been trying to talk to you alone for
ages. You're the only person who can help,"
he babbled, "because you're so smart and
a genius and wonderful... I was only trying
to give you my most precious possessions
with those circuit boards you know – they're
really collectable..."

"Yeah, okay, Nathan, but what IS the matter?"

"You'll have to see for yourself," he said, as we went through the front door and up the stairs.

Dear Diary, walking into Nathan's room was like walking into an alien spaceship. There were just computers everywhere. And parts of computers, and strange circuit board thingies, and widgets and wodgets and gadgets. Cables and inner pieces of computers and computers with *No Eating and Drinking* labels stuck on them... all kinds of computers!

Including the very same computers that were stolen from our school.
!!!

(Sorry, Miss Kinsey.)

I told Bill.

It was too important to do anything else.

He looked at me and said, "Bathsheba, this is very serious. Are you absolutely sure?"

I nodded. "I recognized the *No Eating or Drinking* stickers on them. They're definitely in Nathan's bedroom. He says Jason brought them home and stashed them there."

Then my mouth sort of wobbled, and I said in a rush, "But I don't want Nathan to get in trouble!"

"He won't, I'll make sure of that," Bill said gently. "But I think I need to have a talk with him. Before we call the police."

Sunday evening.

Bill has gone over to the Hunderchunks' house. I begged him to let me come, but he said no way.

I said, "But what if Jason tries to thump you, Da-ad!"

He said, "Well, then I definitely don't want you there, do I?"

"But I wouldn't get in the way!"

"No, but you might get hurt! Tell you what, if you hear screaming, call an ambulance, okay?" He saw the look on my face and said, "I'm joking, Bath! Anyway, I don't think Jason is in. I saw him heading out with those horrible dogs earlier."

DD, I am on tenterhooks! And watching from the window.

All is silence from the Hunderchunk house...

It has been five minutes since he went in there...

Six...

Seven...

Oh no, dear Diary! Here comes Jason! With the horrible dogs! And Dad is still in there!

Oh no, do I call the ambulance right now?
Oh no...

Jason is stopping to let his dogs poop on the lawn...

Dad is still not out...

Oh no, Jason is going to the door...

Fifteen minutes later.

It's okay, panic over! Before I could think about it, I opened the window and yelled, "Dad, Dad, look out!"

Jason turned around to see where the noise was coming from, and JUST at that moment, Bill opened the front door, stepped past him, nodded, smiled and said, "Afternoon," and headed off down the path back toward our house!!!

Jason just stood there with his mouth open, trying to figure out what was going on, and then he yelled at Dad, "Hey, what was you doing in our crib?" Dad said, "Wrong number, man, sorry," over his shoulder, and just kept walking really calmly as if nothing was the matter, back to our house, and let himself in!!!

He is so brave!!

And calm!!!

And cool!!!

I raced downstairs to congratulate him.

"Are you okay, are you okay? You were SPECTACULAR!!!"

"I'm fine! Had a talk with Nathan. You're right – they are the school computers. Looks like Jason and a friend stole them, and he's stashing them in Nathan's room until he can sell them on. Mrs. Hunderchunk's off visiting relatives at the moment, so it's just the two of them. Nathan's terrified of his brother. Poor kid." He looked very serious. "Sounds like his brother makes his life pretty tough sometimes."

I felt terrible. Poor, poor Nathan. I wished I had never mocked his socks.

"What can we do?" I whispered.

"I'll call the police, I suppose."

"But then Jason will know – he'll know Nathan told on him!"

"But what else can I do, Bath?"

"But we can't let Nathan get in trouble," I said, panicking a little.

My brain started to work probably the hardest it has ever worked in its life... All I could think was, *The Bathsheba in the books would know just what to do! Oh, why aren't I more like her? She always has the answer to everything!*

And then all of a sudden, I knew what to do.

"That's it!" I shrieked. "It's all in the books! I mean, the book! I mean, *Bathsheba's Paris Plot!*"

"Bath? What are you talking about?"

"I've got a plan," I said, more calmly. "Leave it to me."

"Come on. How can I do that? We've got to do the right thing."

"But Nathan. He's my – my friend. Please, Dad? Please. It's a great plan. It can't fail."

He sighed.

"Bath? Is this the kind of plan that I would call ridiculous, if I heard it?"

"Um...no, but you might say it was a little Spectacular."

"How did I guess?" he groaned. "Okay – tell me your plan."

After an awful lot of action...

So, dear Diary,
This is what we did.

(If you have read *Bathsheba's Paris Plot*,

you will probably be able to guess!)

We started on the plan about midnight. We wanted to do it as soon as possible, but we also had to be SECRET, and Nathan (who was really into the whole idea) knew Jason was going to a club and probably wouldn't be home until two in the morning.

Bill helped. I couldn't have done it by myself even if he had let me, because I needed him to carry the computers and drive the car. But the idea was all mine!

I put on my blackest clothes and snuck across the street to the Hunderchunks' house while Bill got the car started and moved it over to their side of the road. Everything was dead quiet and the street lights made pools of orange light like spilled Fanta. I knocked quietly on the door, and Nathan opened it at once. He looked at me as if I was a genius or something. "This is such an amazing idea, Bathsheba!" he whispered. "You are a genius!"

"Shush," I said sternly, "we have work to do."

Nathan followed me up the stairs. "This is kind of a date, isn't it?"

"NO, Nathan Hunderchunk, it is NOT! Yuck, yuck, yuck."

I was really worried the dogs might start barking, but Nathan said that he had given them lots of food and shut them in the kitchen, and anyway they were used to strange people coming in late at night, so they never barked unless they were told to. He had also sorted out all the school computers from the rest of the computers and stacked them on the landing.

"I didn't want to keep them," Nathan told me anxiously. "But I didn't know how to get rid of them without Jason killing me. This is the best plan I've ever heard of! You're so clever, Bathsheba! I knew you could fix everything!"

"Stop drooling on my arm," I told him, kindly.

"Okay, Bathsheba! Anything you say! What should I do instead?"

"Are you okay?" Bill came up the stairs. I told him we were fine and he started loading the computers into the car. I ran back downstairs and went outside. I got a brick from the dumpster and wrapped some cloth around it and tried to break the window with it. There was no way I was going to let Bill do all the exciting stuff!

Anyway, it was much harder than I had expected to break the window, and it made a HUGE noise and the glass went everywhere – it was really frightening and I was terrified someone was going to wake up, but no one did. I was really proud I had remembered to break it from the outside, like real burglars would have done.

"You've got to lock yourself in the

bathroom once we've gone," I told Nathan. "You'll have to tell Jason you were really, really scared. And the men who stole the computers had masks on, so you don't know what they looked like."

And then me and Bill drove to the school. With the computers in the back seat.

Dear Diary, you see, the idea is that Jason Hunderchunk will think he has been robbed himself! And then he will not dare go to the police, since the things that were stolen from him he stole himself anyway, just like the stolen stoles the stealers stole! (Ooh, try saying that five times quickly.)

At least I HOPE that is what will happen... It worked for me in *Bathsheba's Paris Plot*! Hopefully it will teach Jason a lesson too.

We unloaded the computers in front of the school gates. Bill had brought some cardboard to cover them with so they just looked like a big pile of trash. And then we drove home. On the way there, we stopped at a pay phone and Bill called the police.

"What did you say?" I asked eagerly.

"Just that there were suspicious characters lurking around the school. I hope they come! And I hope it doesn't rain," he said, poking his head out of the car window.

I looked worriedly at the moon, and it looked worriedly back at me. Rain and things are never a problem in Mother's books. In *Bathsheba's Paris Plot* it was the middle of summer.

When we got home, Bill parked the car and I went inside, yawning. And thinking of poor Nathan, waiting for Jason to come back...

"You go upstairs and get some sleep," Bill told me firmly. "I'll stay up and see what happens when he gets back."

I didn't mean to go to sleep, but I did. Then about an hour later I was woken up by a HOWL of RAGE from the Hunderchunks' house!

I sat up in bed, and shrieked, "Dad, dad, go and see if Nathan is all right!"

"On my way," said Bill, banging out of the front door. I followed him, only stopping to put on my slippers. Bill ran across the street and rang their doorbell. The dogs were whining and barking as if they had been kicked, and I could hear Jason shouting. Bill rang the doorbell again, and Jason wrenched the door open.

"We've been robbed!" he yelled at Bill. Behind him, I could see Nathan on the stairs. Nathan waved.

"That's awful! Want me to call the police?" said Bill.

"Uh...no. No!" Jason suddenly looked really worried. "It's not that bad," he muttered. "They didn't take anything much."

"But still, don't you think...?"

"No police!"

"Suit yourself. We'll get some sleep then."

He took my hand and led me back across the street. I looked back to see Jason, suddenly looking very small and deflated, closing the door.

Wow, dear Diary. I am EXHAUSTED.

I am lying awake with my brain buzzing with thoughts.

What if someone else steals the computers before the police arrive?

What if Jason figures out what went on?

What if...oh, I am too tired, dear Diary! Goodnight!

o o o o o o o o o

Day Thirty-Six
Monday — the final scene!

My heart was in my mouth as I headed to school the next day.

I wasn't just worried about the computers, but about Nathan too!

But thankfully, I didn't have to worry for long. He was standing by the classroom door, looking around nervously. When he saw me he gave me a big grin, so I knew at once everything must be all right.

I ran over. "Nathan, what happened, are you okay?!"

"Yeah, I'm fine. Jason even asked me how I was this morning – I think he was really shocked to get robbed! He hasn't kicked the dogs once today."

I was going to ask about the computers when I heard Keisha calling me. I turned around and saw her running down the hall, looking really excited.

"Bath! You'll never guess! The computers are back!" She slowed down as she saw my face. "Wow, you look exhausted! Are you okay?"

I yawned and grinned at her.

"Bath... What have you been up to?"

"Tell you later," I said. We linked arms and went into the classroom, with Nathan. Everyone was talking about the computers and trying to guess what had happened. I thought how just a few weeks ago I had felt like I was the only person here who was totally lost and confused, and now me and Nathan were the only people who knew what was going on!

I was walking down the hall with Keisha, when two policemen came out of Mr. Baxter-Bix's office. I heard one of them say "fingerprints."

Dear Diary, I just went cold all over.

What if Bill didn't wear gloves?

I tried and tried to remember. Did he have gloves on? I couldn't think.

"Keisha, give me your phone!"

"What, in school? It'll get confiscated!"

"It's an emergency!"

I dialed Bill, my fingers trembling. Miss Kinsey walked past and gave me a stern look.

"Miss Kinsey, if you knew how much of an emergency this was, you would use an exclamation mark," I told her.

Bill answered, sounding really sleepy.

"Did you wear gloves?" I hissed.

"What?"

"Fingerprints! Gloves!"

"Oh, of course, Bath! I've seen a few heist movies too, you know." He laughed.

Keisha stared at me as I gave her the phone back.

"I've got a funny idea I know what you were doing last night, but I can't believe it!"

"No time to tell you now," I said. "We've got to get the Dramarama application e-mailed off and we have just eight hours!"

Dear Diary,
We worked so HARD.

Mr. Baxter-Bix was amazing. He let the drama club all have a day off classes to work with Mr. Trucillo and Miss Kinsey to get the applications ready and e-mailed off.

We still wouldn't have been able to do it if it wasn't for Nathan!

He knew all these amazing computer shortcuts to get the applications put together and looking really cool! We just gazed at him in awe as his fingers flew over the keyboard. Mr. Trucillo said, "Wow, impressive skills, young man!"

Nathan looked so proud of himself.

I said, "Yeah, Nathan, you're a star!" and
I was so happy I actually gave him a hug.

Unfortunately then he went all dizzy, but
he recovered very quickly and we got the
Dramarama applications together – and sent
off – just in time!

And all we can do now, dear Diary, is
WAIT...to find out if me and Keisha have
made it to camp!

Oh no, dear Diary...Keisha.

DD, after all the excitement, I haven't even
thought to tell her about seeing my dad and
Bev kissing!

Is it really my secret to tell?

Well, Keisha is my best friend. And no one
told me not to tell. And I would want to know,
if I were her!

Besides, I have had enough of secrets.

After calling Keisha. ✳

She said, "No way," and then she got really quiet. I wished I was over there so I could see how she really felt, and if she was upset.

"Well, it was just a kiss," I said. "It wasn't really making out."

"Mmm."

"Keish? Are you okay? Keish?"

"Yeah, I'm okay," she said, slowly. "I mean, I really like your dad and everything. It's just—"

"I know," I said. "But oh, Keish, it would be so nice to be your sister."

"You already are my sister," she said, "in every way that counts."

Oh yes, and I did one more thing.

I went over to see Alicia. Because, as much as Keisha's lionessness was awesome, I know Alicia now. And I was sure that she wouldn't be scared off forever.

"I bet you weren't expecting to see me here," I said, when she opened the door.

She folded her arms. "Go on."

"I've got a deal for you," I said. "Well, to be honest, more of a bribe."

"Keep going."

"I don't care what you say about me, but I don't want you to spoil things for Keisha and Rafiq. So here's my deal. If you keep your mouth shut and don't go saying things to their parents – or to anyone! – I will take you to the next highly glamorous party I go to. Because, after all, my mother IS a famous writer. We do, now and then, go to very special book launches. You know, for people like Geri Halliwell, and J.K. Rowling. And you can come too. If you behave."

She smiled her sharp smile, and her eyes glittered.

"Sounds like a deal," she said chirpily.

I hesitated.

"You could be nice, you know," I said. "Why aren't you? We could have been real friends!"

She looked at me in a very superior way.

"If you had any real ambition, Bathsheba," she said, "you'd realize that friends aren't important. What matters is getting what you want."

And she closed the door in my face.

And THAT is the absolute end of my friendship with Alicia. Thank heavens!!!

But the continuation of my best friendship with Keisha, and maybe – if we're lucky – a chance to be even better best friends at Dramarama camp this summer!

o   o   o   o   o   o   o   o   o

THE CLOTBOROUGH SCHOOL GAZETTE

Issue no. 2

A MESSAGE FROM MR. BAXTER-BIX

Following the mysterious return of the school computers, the police were able to identify the thief using modern forensic techniques. The culprit is now under arrest. Many thanks to the students who remained so hard-working and cheerful in this troubled time.

CHRISTMAS RAFFLE

A great idea from one of our newest students: Bathsheba de Trop, who joined this year in Seventh Grade, will be holding a Christmas raffle to raise money to regenerate the playground near her home in Clotborough Estates. Prizes include: a fairy castle bed, a bouncy castle, a giant Snoopy and a piano.

Drama Club's Production Of *Pygmalion*: Laughter, Tears And Song!
By Our Own Correspondent (Miss Kinsey)

Many congratulations to the talented drama club members who put on such a delightful production of that famous comedy, *Pygmalion.* The actors tackled the play with gusto and showed real understanding of its characters. Bathsheba de Trop, in the lead role as Eliza, made a satisfyingly bumptious flower-girl, and got a lot of laughs.

But she also showed another, more vulnerable side to Eliza, as she tried to adjust to her new life as a lady. Her cockney accent was certainly interesting, and occasionally ear-splitting.

Alicia Abebe also deserves particular praise for her acting of Clara, Freddy's bad-tempered sister. Everyone agreed that her catty remarks to Eliza in the first scene were astonishingly convincing.

A special mention must go to the lighting and props teams, too, whose hard work backstage made sure the whole performance ran smoothly and was a joy to watch.

A surprise guest at the performance was celebrity author, Mandy de Trop, who flew in from the USA to watch her daughter act. She kindly signed autographs at intermission. And I have recently received news that suggests that perhaps Bathsheba herself may soon be signing autographs, because I am delighted to announce that she, along with last year's star actress, Keisha Freeman, has won a place at Dramarama camp for the coming summer!

My Top Ten Tips for Surviving School

Dear Diary,

I was really scared when I started school, because I didn't know what to expect. But I survived – yay me! Let me share what I've learned with you...

10) Do not wear a feather boa to school – teachers don't like it.

9) It's really hard trying to find the right classrooms at first, but you get used to it. (Hmm, I wish there was school GPS...)

8) Ties are difficult, but they are like riding a bike – you only have to learn once and then you can do it forever.

7) School clubs are lots of fun, if you find the right one for you!

6) Schools usually have lots of rules – most of them quacko, or designed to stop you from having fun. BUT, mixed in there are some really important ones which Could Save Your Life. It's not always easy to tell which is which...so you probably ought to follow

them all (except the impossible ones, like "Have Your Shirt Tucked In At All Times").

5) That very horrible noise is the bell, and it means you should be somewhere else. Maybe I will start a petition to Mr. Baxter-Bix to get it replaced with a friendlier noise, like a happy lamb going "Baaaa"...

4) If a class is boring, it is really tempting to spend it writing more interesting things under a desk, but it's very embarrassing if you get caught!

3) School is exhausting! Remember to have some fun on the weekends. You deserve it!

2) You don't have to be the very best at every subject — or even at any subject — you should just try your hardest.

1) Being the only new girl in the class can be scary. But remember, you just have to be yourself. Everyone will like you and want to be friends. (Yes they will! Why wouldn't they? You are FANTASTIC!!)

☆ About the author ♡ *

Like Bathsheba's mother, Mandy de Trop, Leila Rasheed is a writer. Unlike Mandy, Leila lives in Birmingham, England. This is not as glamorous as Kensington in London, but it does have a suburb called Hollywood!

Here are some more differences between Mandy and Leila:

☆ Mandy has a diamond-encrusted swimming pool to splash around in.

☆ Leila just has a bathtub to splash around in, which is lucky, as she loves bubble-baths (and Bathsheba!).

☆ Mandy rides around in swishy, dishy limousines.

☆ Leila rides around on buses and trains. She loves walking too — you can explore a lot more on foot than from behind the tinted windows of a limo.

- Mandy has a housekeeper to clean up after her.
- Leila lives with a saxophonist, who sometimes cleans up, but mostly makes weird and wonderful music.

- Mandy writes in a perfectly white office, where nobody is allowed to touch anything in case it gets dirty.
- Leila writes in a jumble of computer cables, cookie crumbs and half-empty mugs of tea.

- Mandy is often to be found surrounded by fans pleading for her autograph.
- Leila is often to be found surrounded by notebooks full of scribbled ideas for new stories, silently pleading to be written.

☆ **What everyone thought about Bathsheba's first** ✳
⑥ **fantastic diary...** ♭

Chips, Beans and Limousines

"*Chips, Beans and Limousines* is a brilliant and imaginative book. It made me laugh out loud but it also made me think. It is a 5* read, I loved it!!!!!!" Jessica

"I love this book and I would definitely recommend it." Kirsty

"A fun read – loved it from the first page!!" Megan

"After I read this book I knew just what to write my 'Favorite Book Report' on." Mabel

Find out what Bathsheba Clarice de Trop does next...

Bathsheba finds new friends, an old enemy, and lots of excitement at Dramarama camp!

But will she really be good enough to appear on Dramarama Diaries?

Find out in

Doughnuts, Dreams and Drama Queens

Out now!

For Mum and Dad and Shafiq,
with love.

First published in 2008 by Usborne Publishing Ltd., Usborne House,
83-85 Saffron Hill, London EC1N 8RT, England.
www.usborne.com

Copyright © Leila Rasheed, 2008
The right of Leila Rasheed to be identified as the author of this work has been
asserted by her in accordance with the Copyright, Designs and Patents Act, 1988.

Illustration page 5 by Lee Wildish.
Other inside illustrations by Vicky Arrowsmith.

The name Usborne and the devices ♀ ⊕ are Trade Marks of Usborne Publishing Ltd.

A CIP catalogue record for this book is available from the British Library.

UK ISBN 9780746098851 First published in America in 2011. AE
American ISBN 9780794530297

JF AMJJASOND/11 00182/1

Printed in Reading, Berkshire, UK.